Also by M. K. Wren
Published by Ballantine Books:

CURIOSITY DIDN'T KILL THE CAT

A MULTITUDE OF SINS

OH, BURY ME NOT

NOTHING'S CERTAIN BUT DEATH

SEASONS
OF DEATH

M. K. Wren

BALLANTINE BOOKS • NEW YORK

Library of Congress Catalog Card Number: 80-2082

ISBN 0-345-35003-0

Manufactured in the United States of America

First Ballantine Books Edition: January 1990

With thanks to Mildretta and Walt Adams
and Ed Jagels of Silver City, Idaho—
stewards of the memory and
champions of the dream . . .

CHAPTER 1

Ten miles east of Drewsey, the Oregon State Highway Department had thoughtfully put up a sign—white on green in this sienna and ochre landscape—to advise motorists that they were crossing from Pacific to mountain standard time and should set their clocks ahead one hour.

Conan Flagg held the steering wheel with his left hand while he adjusted his watch: 8:36 June 12. The Jaguar XK-E thrummed effortlessly along a lonely, sagebrush-lined highway under a sun that burned hot even this early in the day. His passage stirred the only wind, a miniature fifty-five-mile-an-hour gale that tossed his hair, black as the sleek Jaguar, black as his eyes behind the dark glasses. The Indian slant was emphasized by his reflexive squint; he was traveling straight into the sun's glare.

Conan looked out at the arid, sage-velveted hills, rank on rank, the basalt mesas layered with blood-brown flows, millennia deep, and he experienced one of those moments when something within him roused to demand: *what am I doing here?*

Murder. That was the answer, and it seemed vaguely unreal as the erosion-razed landscape spun past him.

A murder had occurred on a chill autumn night forty years

ago, and that was why he was driving into the sun on this warm summer morning and had spent most of the previous day behind this wheel.

Nearly four hundred miles behind him, across the breadth of the state of Oregon, the sun would be making mist in pine and spruce forests and glinting on silk and cream breakers, but he wasn't there to look out the windows of his house to see them. Nor was he there to walk the two blocks to the ramshackle, shingled pile that he regarded as his one contribution to the continuity of civilization: the Holliday Beach Book Shop. He wasn't there for Miss Beatrice Dobie's inevitable "Good morning, Mr. Flagg," nor for Meg's hoarse, Siamese complaints about the tardiness of her breakfast.

Conan Flagg wasn't there because in his billfold he carried a card that proclaimed him a licensed private investigator, and because forty years ago a man named Leland Langtry had died when a knife was driven into his heart.

Conan leaned into the wheel around a long curve and looked southeast over a tumble of arid hills. He couldn't see the Owyhee Mountains, not yet; they were still two hours beyond the horizon and across the state line in Idaho. On the road map, the Owyhees lurked in the extreme southwest corner of Idaho, and there was little else in that corner: few roads, few rivers, and only a handful of tiny circles designating towns with populations of zero to five hundred.

One of those circles bore the name of Silver City.

That had once been a stellar name in the history of the West. The first gold was found in 1863, then the fabulous lodes of the metal that gave the town its name. In the following decades, a cornucopia of silver flowed from its mines and mills surpassed in quantity only by the Comstock lode of Nevada.

Conan had learned all that from history books in his library, which had also informed him that by 1942 Silver City was in its death throes, the mines deserted, the labyrinthine miles of tunnels left to drown in seeping groundwater or collapse with the rotting of their timbers; the huge stamp mills that once stair-stepped down the mountains, their pounding roar echoing along the valleys, were dismantled, carried off piece by piece, the solid tons of cast-iron machinery melted down to make howitzers and tanks. Now Silver City stood eroding on the high, dry shoulders of the Owyhees, and only its history kept it alive.

But in 1940 the town was still living by its silver, even if only a few mines and one mill showed vital signs and the end was in sight. And in that year Leland Langtry met his end, and his body was hidden in a deserted, boarded-up mine tunnel.

That didn't come out of the histories, but from a letter that had reached Conan's desk at the Holliday Beach Book Shop the day before yesterday. With the letter was a clipping dated June 3 from Boise's *Idaho Statesman* headlined, "Verdict Reached on Ghost Town Murder." The story behind the murder, as recounted by the *Statesman*, began in Silver City on the night of September 22, 1940, when Leland Langtry, a partner in the Lang-Star Mining Company, disappeared, and with him his car, his secretary, Amanda Count, and $10,000 in Lang-Star company funds. The police search continued for months, but neither Langtry, the car, Amanda Count, nor the money were found, and it was assumed at the time that Langtry had stolen the money and departed in the car with his secretary, with whom he had had a long-standing extramarital love affair. It was Langtry who was married; Amanda Count, less than half his age, was single.

Then on May 14 of this year, a Bureau of Land Management survey party had opened an old mine adit near Silver City and discovered the skeletal remains of a man subsequently identified as Leland Langtry. The cause of death was apparently stabbing: a knife was still wedged between the fifth and sixth ribs just left of the sternum, where it had without a doubt—according to the medical testimony at the Owyhee County coroner's inquest—pierced the heart.

The consensus of the jury was that Langtry had indeed planned to abscond with the Lang-Star funds and his secretary, but had been discovered in process of the theft by his partner, Thomas Starbuck, who had been so outraged he responded by stabbing Langtry to death. The murder weapon, the knife, was known to belong to Starbuck and was marked with his initials. The subsequent fate of the money and the secretary remained a mystery, but the jury reached its verdict with scant delay: they expressed their sympathy for the motive by calling it second-degree manslaughter, but apparently had no reservations in pointing a collective finger at Thomas Starbuck as the perpetrator of the crime.

But Starbuck would never be convicted; he would never be tried. In 1955 Thomas Starbuck had died of cancer of the liver.

As far as Owyhee County was concerned, justice was done; the murder of Leland Langtry could be comfortably relegated to history. But there was one dissenting opinion, and it reached Conan Flagg via the letter that accompanied the clipping.

. . . I am well aware that this murder is forty years old and the accused man died a quarter of a century ago, but is there a time limit on justice? Tom Starbuck did not—could not—commit this crime, and justice demands that his name be cleared. He was a good man who worked hard all his life to make a better life for those he loved. He does not deserve to be remembered as a murderer. . . .

Cordelia Becket Starbuck, widow of the accused, wrote with the crafted, regular hand of another generation, one in which the lost art of penmanship was integral to a child's education; a generation in which dignity and restraint were considered virtues to be cultivated.

. . . Mr. Flagg, you are my last resort, and I am grateful to your aunt Dolly for suggesting that I appeal to you. I can't simply surrender Tom's good name without exhausting every possibility. Beyond that, there is another consideration—if Tom is innocent, then somebody else is guilty. That person also deserves justice. . . .

Conan couldn't deny the efficacy of that argument, but his initial response on reading the letter was annoyance, not at Cordelia Starbuck, but at Dolly Flagg.

Conan's aunt Dolly liked to think of herself as mistress of the Ten-Mile Ranch. Conan might still be majority stockholder—he had in fact been sole heir to that mini-empire upon his father's premature death—and Dolly's son Avery might be the chairman of the board and the one who actually ran the incorporated ranch, but Dolly persisted in playing the role of the *grande dame*. She also considered it obligatory to that role to keep herself fully up to date on the activities, however personal, of everyone connected with the Ten-Mile, and her correspondence—which Conan privately characterized as her newsletters—reached the most remote places of the planet, but especially her "neighbors" in eastern Oregon, Washington, and Idaho. That Conan was a card-carrying private investigator was a fact he did not like advertised. He could afford to be selective about the cases he undertook, and preferred to do his own selecting. He had so informed Dolly on numerous occasions, but to no avail.

He was thus somewhat biased against Mrs. Starbuck's case at the outset, although he had to admit it piqued his curiosity. But it was hopeless. What could he do after forty years that the law enforcement agencies of Idaho could not?

When he reached Mrs. Starbuck by telephone—which took some time; there were only two telephones in Silver City, one at the Idaho Hotel, the other at the General Store—he had every intention of politely but firmly refusing her case. Yet here he was, a long drive from his seaside home on his way to Silver City to undertake an investigation that was bound to be fruitless. He wasn't exactly sure how she had so deftly changed his mind for him, but no doubt Cordelia Starbuck—Delia, she said; she preferred to be called Delia—was not accustomed to having her requests denied.

At eleven-thirty Conan crossed the state line into Idaho near the point where the Snake River, after traversing the width of the state, turns north. The Snake had once been a legendary river that inspired awe and fear, but it had been dammed into submission now, its mountain-born waters diverted into millions of irrigation ditches that created a verdant oasis like a garland across the lower half of Idaho. For thirty miles the highway skirted the southern verge of that fertile swath. Lush pastures and fields of corn, sugar beets, onions, and potatoes flashed past on Conan's left, but on the other side of the highway, beyond the barbed-wire fences, the desert waited always.

And beyond the desert, the Owyhee Mountains.

They were no longer below the horizon now; they made up more than half his horizon. They loomed in his vision and in his mind, constantly drawing his gaze away from the gray ribbon of the highway, and finally the highway, as if it also felt the mysterious attraction, turned south, leaving the long oasis behind.

The name "Owyhee," according to some historians, derived from "Hawaii," and indeed both were accented similarly. That exotic association was traced to the 1840s when two native Hawaiians employed as trappers for Hudson's Bay Company passed through the area. Conan accepted that explanation for no other reason than that he relished the very improbability of it. This was a land of improbabilities. The miles spun monotonously under his wheels as the sun neared zenith. The air had the dry scent of a kiln, and mirages of water shone on the asphalt ahead. At length, he saw a dark, tree-fringed island suspended above a shimmering lake. That would be Murphy, the Owyhee County seat.

As he approached, the lake disappeared and the dark island settled firmly on the ground, but there was still something unlikely about it. The entire town with its population of seventy-five—according to the road sign—was built on the right side of the highway, clustered around a dignified, one-story, brick building of WPA vintage: the Owyhee County courthouse.

Conan didn't stop to examine this seat of government more closely. He would be back. The county sheriff's office was there.

He stayed on the highway for another five miles until he saw a sign pointing southwest toward the Owyhees. "Silver City 23 miles." He turned right onto a rutted gravel road striking bravely across a plateau gray with stunted sagebrush no more than a foot in height, mute witness on this summer day to the bitter winds of winter. Over the plateau the Owyhees brooded, a barren, serrated, and cleft mass forged under the incandescent foundations of the continent and possessed of a strangely serene savagery. These granite eminences bore the sky on their shoulders and commanded the clouds. Conan sought the blunted peak that loomed highest in the range: War Eagle Mountain. On its western flank, little more than a thousand feet below its summit, he would find Silver City. At the moment, that seemed incredible.

It seemed even more incredible by the time he reached the town. That twenty-three miles took nearly an hour and a half to traverse. The road hair-pinned endlessly like a topographic map line, threading the contours of gully and gulch in a continuous, insecure notch above vertiginous drops. In the lower elevations, steep talus slopes were stained with plutonic bursts of red, yellow, and orange; bluffs of basalt rose above and below him, ominous umber black frosted with acid green lichen. But the heights were the realm of granite, that ancient and most steadfast of rock, surrendering so slowly to the inevitable forces of erosion that it seemed to the human mind immutable. The desert scrub was superceded by juniper, and along the creeks cottonwoods and dense thickets of shrubby willows flourished, and chokecherries and serviceberries bloomed. On the high ridges, the road wound through copses of the graceful, tough little mountain mahogany and stands of Douglas and subalpine fir, where in the shadows at their feet bluebells bloomed.

Conan found himself eating his own dust time and again as the road turned on itself, and he found himself swearing aloud time and again while he eased the XK-E over granite hummocks exposed by the last gully washer. Yet as the miles fell in convoluted loops behind him, he felt a growing exhilaration, a quickening of his senses. These mountains, because of the precious ores they held bound, had been explored and exploited for well over a century, yet it seemed an untouched, primeval world impervious even to time. He had the feeling that at the end of this tortuous trail he would find some sort of occidental Shangri-la.

Finally, he descended from one more summit into a deep valley, and near the bank of the stream that had cut it, reached a junction. A crude sign pointed west to DeLamar and south to Silver City. He took the left-hand road, which wound along the gravel beds skirting the stream. That would be Jordan

Creek. Further down its course the first gold had been panned from its waters 117 years ago.

He passed two small buildings with stout stone walls. Powder houses, undoubtedly, for storing dynamite. On an open slope on the other side of the creek, he saw a cemetery, its white markers leaning back slightly into the hill. Then he rounded a curve and realized he had reached his destination. Ahead on his right were the first houses, precariously hugging the slope, front porches clinging to the edge of the road. A signboard announced:

> WELCOME TO SILVER CITY, IDAHO
> ALL PROPERTY IS PRIVATELY OWNED
> PLEASE DO NOT DESTROY OR TRESPASS
> VIOLATORS WILL BE PROSECUTED
>   —OWYHEE COUNTY SHERIFF

War Eagle Mountain held magnificent dominion over the town, tawny flanks intersecting the blue of the sky in vast curves rising to their vertex in the southeast, a little to Conan's left. From this point he could see perhaps thirty structures, most roofed in silvery or rust-red corrugated metal with walls of wood weathered a rich, golden brown, and he was struck then, as he would be many times again, by the serendipitous arrangements of color and texture, of vertical, horizontal, and diagonal. To his left, solitary on a high slope, stood one of the few painted buildings, a little church shining benignly white in the sun. Conan had stopped the car, and now he realized he was smiling. No Shangri-la this, but something about it lifted the spirits; a sense of surprise, of discovery.

That there were man-made structures—and these were undeniably not only man-made but *hand*made—in these mountains was in itself amazing, and it was astounding to realize that these were only remnants of a human community whose population had once numbered in the thousands; a lively, doughty community that had been the county seat when Idaho was still a territory; had been the terminus of its first telegraph service; and even before the turn of the century, had been lighted by electricity produced in one of Idaho's first hydroelectric plants; had its own school, newspaper, brewery, and cigar factory; its own hospital and water system; and had produced and shipped out via stagecoach and horse- or ox-drawn freight wagon silver and gold bullion literally by the ton.

And while Silver City might be called a ghost town, it could not be called deserted. Conan counted four people ahead at what seemed to be the center of town, as well as three parked cars and a pickup. He shifted into first gear as the road sloped down to Jordan Creek, which made a short dogleg under the road before resuming its north-south course. There was no bridge, only a dirt fill over a huge culvert, then a rising slope, and finally the road leveled in front of a long, rambling wooden building whose most notable feature was the porch fronting its two stories along its entire length. On the upper level of the porch the floor sagged dramatically, and Conan had to admire the daring of the two people working there.

The building was, he saw when he reached it, the Idaho Hotel, and not only in process of repair and restoration, but open for business. At least, a sign advertised soft drinks, beer, candy, cigarettes, display rooms, and food. The daring ones on the upper level of the porch were wielding hammers enthusiastically on the railing, and Conan doubted either of them was yet twenty years old. The same could be said of one of the two men supervising from the street, but the other was old enough to be a father to any or all of them. His dark hair was shoulder length, and he sported a full beard, a high-crowned Stetson, and tall leather boots. He watched curiously as the car approached, and when Conan stopped, he smiled and said, "Howdy."

Conan refrained from raising an eyebrow at that. "Hello. I wonder if you could tell me how to find Cordelia Starbuck's house."

"Delia's? Sure. You must be Mr. Flagg."

Conan did raise an eyebrow at that. "Well, yes, I am."

"Jake Kulik," the man responded, putting out a hand. Then, indicating the young man standing beside him, "This here's my son, John." John's smile was very much like his father's and his hair was the same dark brown, but cut a few inches shorter. "And up there," Kulik continued, waving toward the porch, where the hammering had ceased, "That's Laurie Franklin and Bill Cobb, friends of John's."

Both Laurie and Bill, blithely bare-legged and bare-armed in the searing sun, offered easy smiles with the amenities, and Laurie had a few questions about the XK-E. ("Wow! They don't even *make* those anymore.") And finally Kulik got down to the business of directions.

"Well, you just keep right on down Jordan Street here, past those two poplars, then turn left at the first street. It'll take you over the crick, then it runs into Morning Star Street. Take another left there, then when you get to the school-house—it's that big, gray building. . . ." He was gesturing toward the hotel now, as if Conan could see through it, "turn right and go up the hill. The Starbuck house'll be right in front of you. Biggest, fanciest house in Silver; the one with all the gingerbread and the big arch over the upstairs balcony. You can't miss it."

Conan thanked him and drove off in the indicated direction, noting in passing the white Cadillac parked near the end of the porch. It seemed out of place here. And in a way it was: it had California license plates.

He had no trouble following Kulik's directions. For one thing, the Starbuck house—now that he had it identified—was visible from almost any point in the town, occupying as it did a commanding vantage on the slopes east of Jordan Creek. It was two stories high and of imposing proportions, ornamented with scalloped shingles and whimsies of gingerbread in an oddly blunt, geometric style. One wing of the roof jutted forward to cover the balcony above the front porch—the balcony that Kulik had noted, with its wide, fretted arch—and the porch itself extended on the right into a veranda that went around the side of the house. The roof was the silvery, corrugated metal that seemed the material of choice here—at least, for the buildings that *had* roofs—but unlike most of the others, this house was painted: an ivory yellow trimmed in ochre, with decorative details picked out in sky blue. Three crab apple trees, resplendent in white blossoms, stood before the house, but separated from it by a barren dirt expanse.

When Conan turned in just beyond the trees, he saw a man and woman talking together at the foot of the porch steps, and another woman leaning against a post at the top of the steps. The latter didn't move, nor did the man, but when Conan parked in the scented shade of the crab apples, the other woman started toward him.

"Mr. Flagg?"

He got out of the car, stretching out the stiffness in his legs, and he was a little surprised that his mental image of Cordelia Becket Starbuck agreed so well with the lady herself.

She was eighty years old—she'd told him that in their telephone conversation; "born with this century"—yet she stood tall and straight and walked with assurance, and her hair, combed into a loose bun at the back of her head, was only salted with gray. She wore a simple dress with a conservative print, blue on beige, with low-heeled shoes and hose. The price of years was in her face, but it could not detract from her handsome features—high cheekbones, a wide brow that in another age would be called noble, and clear, gray eyes that in any age would be called beautiful.

Conan took the hand she offered. "Mrs. Starbuck?"

"Delia. Welcome to Silver. I didn't expect you so early. You didn't drive all the way today?"

Like so many people who hadn't grown up with the car, she had rather a vague concept of distances. "No, I stayed last night with some friends at the Black Stallion Ranch."

"The McFalls?" She nodded. "I knew Carlotta years ago before she married Aaron. What a pity she died so young. Well, you must have a suitcase somewhere in that little car."

He smiled at that and got his suitcase out of the trunk along with the combination-locked briefcase. Delia eyed that curiously. "Looks like you carry your own safe."

"Just the tools of my trade," he replied lightly. That included fingerprinting equipment, evidence envelopes, microscope slides, lock picks, a 12 × magnifying glass, binoculars, camera, infrared scope, tape recorder, and a Mauser 9 mm automatic. Habit, he thought ruefully; bringing this briefcase had only been a matter of habit. It was very unlikely that any of this equipment would be of any use to him on this case—not when forty years had elapsed to obliterate the kind of evidence these tools were designed to uncover or preserve.

When she offered to carry the briefcase, he surrendered it and walked with her toward the house. Since his arrival he had been the object of a penetrating scrutiny by the man who still stood at the foot of the porch steps. Conan judged him to be in his sixties, a lean, leathery man with a Lincolnesque face and prominent browridges over dark eyes. He was studying Conan from beneath those lowering brows with an intentness that gave him a peculiarly lugubrious aspect.

Delia said, "Mr. Flagg, I'd like you to meet an old and dear friend, Dexter Adler. He just drove up from Boise." That explained his attire, a well-tailored brown silk suit, which obviously hadn't come off a ready-to-wear rack. Delia added, "Dex was a friend of Tom's, too."

Dexter Adler was not, apparently, prepared to be a friend of Conan Flagg's. He didn't offer a hand or put aside his frown. "Mr. Flagg, I might as well say it right out—I think this investigation business is . . ." He glanced defensively at Delia. "Well, it's just damnfoolishness! I'm sorry, Delia, but as much as I liked Tom—and you know I did—all the investigating in the world won't change a thing. Leave it *alone*, Delia—please!"

Her chin came up, but her smile was tolerant, even sympathetic. "Dex, my mind is made up. You know that."

"But what in God's green earth does it *matter* after all these years?"

She responded with steadfast dignity, "It matters." A pause, then, "You'd better have supper with us, Dex. You must be tired out, and there's probably nothing but canned beans in your pantry."

"Uh . . . thanks, but I brought some groceries with me." The look he gave Conan was almost accusing, as if Conan were purposely barring him from Delia's table. "Better get 'em put away and the house opened up. I'll talk to you later,

Delia. Good-bye, Clare." That was for the woman at the top of the steps, who smiled wanly and waved a small hand.

Delia watched him stalk away around the north corner of the house, then she started up the steps, shaking her head. "Mr. Flagg, that is one of the most considerate men I've ever known. He's just not himself today. Well, we'd better get you settled. But first—" She slipped her arm around the other woman's waist. "—I want you to meet my sister."

At close range, the familial resemblance was obvious, but of the two sisters, this had been the beauty, and, Conan thought, she must have been stunning. Her features were fine and perfectly proportioned, her eyes, gray like Delia's, were large and long-lashed and had about them a disarming ingenuousness. Her hair was entirely white, although Conan guessed her to be younger than Delia. He didn't have to guess that she had been very conscious of her beauty; she still was. The rouge and bright lipstick, the showy jewelry, the whispy curls framing her face, and the ribbon binding her long hair at the nape of her neck were all poignant evidence of that.

Conan offered his hand, which she took tentatively as Delia completed the introduction. "Clare, this is Conan Flagg. Mr. Flagg, my sister, Clare Langtry."

"Lang—" Conan swallowed the word, but cast a questioning look at Delia, who frowned briefly, then nodded.

"I guess I didn't tell you. Yes, Clare was Leland Langtry's wife."

Conan felt distinctly awkward. He said to Clare, "I'm sorry about your husband, Mrs. Langtry."

The long lashes swept down, then up again as she presented a smile. "Nobody calls me 'Mrs. Langtry' anymore. It's just 'Clare.' And don't worry about Lee. He always comes—"

"Clare," Delia cut in, "would you mind fixing some iced tea while I take Mr. Flagg upstairs?" She crossed to the front door, pausing when she saw Conan ready to open it. "Have you had lunch, Mr. Flagg?"

"It's just 'Conan' for me—please. And lunch would be most welcome." He held the door for the sisters, then followed them into a sitting room that was small but still light and airy with its four windows. To his right a pair of wicker chairs flanked an electric floor lamp with an ornate brass base, but on a small table near the door he saw a kerosene stand lamp, which made him wonder about the source of electricity here, and that in turn made him aware of a low droning from outside the house. A generator, undoubtedly; he'd seen no power lines coming into Silver City.

Delia led the way into a wainscoted hall where the dim light reminded Conan to take off his sunglasses. On his left, louvered doors were folded back to give him a glimpse of a living room, which, he speculated, the sisters probably called the parlor, and directly across the hall another set of louvered doors were open on a dining room with a wide bay window. Clare disappeared behind the door at the end of the hall, while Delia started up the staircase on the left-hand wall. Conan's hand went automatically to the sphere atop the newel post, and he wondered how many generations of hands doing exactly the same thing had brought the wood to its present satin polish.

"How old is the house, Delia?"

"Well, different parts are different ages, but Asa Starbuck started it about 1870. That was Tom's grandfather. He was the first Starbuck in Silver. Did well for himself, but that wasn't so hard in those days."

The stairs made a right-angle turn onto a small landing where there was a closed door that Conan guessed gave access to the back rooms of the house. Then another turn, a few more steps, and another hall. Delia passed the doors on either side and proceeded to the one at the end of the hall.

"I'm afraid it's awfully small," she said as she put his briefcase down inside the door. "This used to be a sun porch. Tom's mother always liked to call it a solarium."

Conan deposited his suitcase at the foot of a narrow bed covered with a crocheted spread to which someone had devoted untold hours with the expectation that it would be used by generations to come. The mahogany headboard, waxed to a fine glow, was edged in a carved egg-and-dart motif, and on either side of it kerosene bracket lamps with bases and shades of opaque rose-hued glass were mounted. Conan smiled as he looked around at the pale yellow wainscoting and the faded wallpaper above, with its narrow, flowered stripes. On the wall opposite the hall door were two windows separated by another door. He opened it, and there was the balcony with the gingerbread-bordered arch framing a vista of the town against a backdrop of mountains and incredibly blue sky.

"Delia, this is exactly the room I'd have chosen for myself."

She smiled, pleased. "That balcony is the best thing old Asa ever did for this house. That's why we decided to use this for a guest room. We've got six bedrooms, all told, but we can't keep all of them up, and we don't need them, just the two of us. There's even one for servants downstairs." She shook her head ruefully. "It's been a long time since there were servants here, but that bedroom comes in handy as a pantry. The Roseberrys close the grocery in the winter, so we have to stock up for at least five months."

"You and Clare spend the winters here?"

No doubt his incredulity showed, and she laughed. "Of course. This is our home. Where else would we spend the winters?"

"Does anyone else winter over in Silver City?"

"Oh, sometimes Jake Kulik does. He owns the Idaho Hotel. By the way, we don't have electricity up here on the second floor yet. If it weren't for that generator Dex got us a few years ago, we wouldn't have it *down*stairs. *Nor* water piped into the house. We've got a good well, but we couldn't get water inside without the pump." Then she added wryly, "It's almost like the old days before the power company came in and tore down the lines, and the water system finally broke down. We've even got an *in*side bathroom now. It's downstairs by the kitchen. Well, I'll give you a chance to unpack." She frowned at her watch. "I've got some dough rising I'll have to check. And I'd better see how Clare's coming along."

Conan had the feeling the last was less of an excuse than a real concern. From downstairs came the sound of a screaming tea kettle, then the crash of breaking glass.

CHAPTER 2

Conan was served lunch in the dining room with Clare fluttering around him, her overwhelming attentiveness making him uncomfortable. Delia stayed in the kitchen, pleading necessity. "The dough's ready, and I've *got* to get it in the oven." Conan couldn't object if it meant more bread like that enclosing his roast beef sandwich.

Clare kept eyeing him curiously but covertly, which didn't make him feel any more comfortable, but he understood her interest. At least he thought he did until she asked cautiously, "Didn't Delia say you were Henry Flagg's son?"

He shrugged. "She probably did, since I am."

"Oh." A pause while she looked at his face. "I met Henry Flagg once. That was a long time ago; he was still a young man. You . . . don't look at all like him."

Conan laughed, and now he *did* understand. Apparently Clare found it difficult to correlate Henry Flagg's fair, typically Irish features and red hair with his son's dark, typically—and undeniably—Indian features and black hair.

He explained, "My mother was Nez Percé. In fact, she gave me my middle name: Joseph."

Clare looked momentarily blank, then brightened. "Oh—after *Chief* Joseph? Well."

She let the matter of his ancestry drop, and he wasn't sure whether that was due to the uneasiness with non-Caucasian races that people of her generation and background so often seemed to feel, or simply to lack of interest, and except for that, their conversation was limited to such deep subjects as a comparison of the climates of the Owyhees and the Oregon coast. At one point, he asked her bluntly, "You know why I'm here, don't you?"

She refilled his iced tea glass, frowning slightly, then with an engaging smile asked, "Are you ready for dessert? Delia makes the most elegant pound cake. . . ."

He didn't pursue the subject of his purpose, and after lunch when he was ushered into the parlor—and Clare did, indeed, call it that—he learned with some relief that her assistance was required in the kitchen. He settled into a capacious arm-chair to light a cigarette—the ashtray on the table by his chair assured him smoking was tolerated—and to study the room.

Asa Starbuck had spared no pains here. From the coffered ceiling hung a brass chandelier bearing six lamps with amber Tiffany shades. On the parquet floor was an exquisite Kir-man, and the fireplace on the interior wall was decorated with tile cast in bird and animal forms. Centered on the north wall opposite the fireplace was a double window curtained with lace, and on its wide sill an array of potted plants flour-ished even in the north light. Conan wondered which of the sisters had the green thumb. There had been potted plants in every room he'd seen.

A couch faced the fireplace and at each end a wing chair angled in to form a conversational grouping. Conan occupied one of these chairs, but now he rose and wandered over to the upright piano on the west wall. The dark wood was like silk to his touch, richly carved with entwined leaves and flowers, and he considered how this instrument had reached Silver City. Probably by ship from the east around the Horn to Portland, by barge up the Columbia, by rail to Boise or Murphy, then the tortuous haul through the Owyhees in a wagon pulled by fourteen horses at the command of a jerkline skinner. What price music? And he mentally took his hat off to the people who were willing to pay that price.

He crossed to the big rolltop desk to the right of the double windows, ran his fingers down the ridged curve of the cover with more than a little envy, then turned to study the bookshelves that filled the east wall to a height of five feet. The books ranged from rare editions on geology and mining to recent best sellers, primarily nonfiction. The top of the shelves was given over to memorabilia—family photographs, albums, a pipe stand, three military medals from World War I. His eye was caught by a piece of rock, which seemed incongruous here. It fit solidly in his hand; flecks of mica glittered amid patches of pale feldspar, but it was composed predominantly of a nearly translucent, reddish mineral that seemed on the verge of crystalization.

"That's what it was all about, this town." Delia was coming in through the louvered doors on the other side of the fireplace. She crossed to him, nodding at the rock. "Ruby silver. I guess the proper name is pyrargyrite or proustite."

"This is silver ore?"

"Yes. That's what people have been digging for and fighting over in these mountains since the Civil War."

"It looks harmless enough." He put the rock back in its place, then noting Delia's eye straying to the photographs propped on the shelf, he asked, "Your family?"

"Yes. Gets to be quite a gallery at my age. That's Tom junior, our oldest boy." She laughed at herself. "Well, hardly a boy. Losing his hair and getting a middle-aged spread. Growing up with rocks and mines rubbed off on him; he studied geology, and now he's in Washington, D.C., with the U. S. Geological Survey. These are his daughters, Karèn and Lisa, and his son, Doug; he's at Boston University. This is our daughter Kathleen with her husband, Jim Spalding. He runs a farm down on the Snake near Nyssa. This is their son, Peter, and Hugh, my *great*-grandchild. Now, *that'll* make you feel your years. And here's Kathy and Jim's daughter, Pam; she teaches fifth grade in Boise. Isn't she pretty? The image of Clare when she was young." Delia paused then, looking anxiously toward the door.

When she met Conan's questioning look, she shrugged and said, "I was just wondering about Clare. I don't like to go on about my kids if she's around to hear. It's . . . sort of a tender subject with her."

"Tender? May I ask why?"

Delia gave him an oblique glance. "Well, I suppose you'll have to ask a lot of questions about things that might otherwise be private. It's tender because Clare couldn't have children. She had three miscarriages, and the last one nearly killed her. She always thought it would've made a lot of difference if she and Lee had kids. Anyway, this is a more interesting gallery up here." She looked up at the photographs on the wall above the shelves, most mounted behind glass in narrow, black frames. "Some of these are the only copies left."

The photographs were all old, all depicting subjects related to Silver City and mining. There were several views of the entire town taken at different periods, chronicling its rise and fall. The oldest was dated 1868.

"Now, this one—" Delia pointed to a photograph showing a group of men posing in four ranks before a wooden building. "This was the crew of the Trade Dollar mine, and this man here in the back row, that's Big Bill Haywood."

Conan raised an eyebrow. "Of Wobbly fame?"

"That's him. Got his start right here in Silver back in the nineties. These are some of the mills. Lord, the noise they made, and we never thought a thing about it. That's the Ida Elmore, the Potosi, the Morning Star, and this is the Lang-Star mill."

Conan leaned closer to examine that one. Like the others, it was an immense building, stairstepping down a hillside under long, angled sweeps of roof that gave it an oddly contemporary aspect.

"If you look out the window, you can see where it was," Delia said, going to the double window and lifting one sash. Then, when Conan joined her: "There beyond the church on the hill, that pile of tailings—the mill was right there."

Conan looked out at the mountainous drift of white rock

where chaparral and mountain mahogany found a foothold now and tried to imagine the busy, rumbling mill there.

"How far away is it, Delia?"

"Oh, about a quarter of a mile. Used to be a good road up to it."

There was little between the house and the mine site now except gullied, sagebrush-covered slopes and a few widely separated houses. One, a small frame house with a steep roof, was only a hundred yards away. Conan's attention was called to it by the new Jeep Cherokee parked beside it.

He asked, "Is that Dex Adler's house?"

"Yes. I think he keeps it mainly out of sentiment. That was the house he and Irene had when they lived here. Dex lives in Boise now. He's in real estate."

"Irene is his wife?"

"Was. She died—oh, I guess it was in forty-two. So much happened that year. The mill went bankrupt, and we lost our youngest boy, Howard. Polio. Nobody seems to remember now about polio, how terrifying it was."

Conan hesitated, then, "I guess people have too many other terrors to deal with. When did Dex live here?"

"Well, he came in nineteen thirty-five, I think, and moved to Boise in forty-two. He was the bookkeeper for Lang-Star."

"So, he was here at the time of Lee's murder. Delia, why is he so opposed to an investigation?"

She rested her hands on the sill, frowning. "Oh, I guess he thinks the past is best left alone. Besides, that was an unhappy time for him. Maybe he just doesn't want to be reminded of it. By the way, that next house—the one with the porch across the front—that was Clare and Lee's."

The house she pointed out was a short distance from Adler's and on the same level on the hillside. Delia added, "Clare moved in with us after Lee disappeared, but it was ten years before Tom and I could talk her into selling the house. She kept waiting for Lee to come home. In fact, she still—" Delia broke off suddenly, and a moment later Conan understood why. Clare came into the room carrying a tray with a pitcher of iced tea and glasses. She wore a wide-brimmed straw hat tied under her chin with a pink sash, and her full skirt fluttered as she swept in, smiling, and put the tray down on a table by the couch.

"I thought you might like some more tea. Oh, dear, it is *so* warm today. More like August than June."

Delia went to the tray and began filling the glasses. "Thank you, Clare. Well, just remember, the sun's good for the garden. Tea, Conan?"

"Yes, thanks." He crossed to her to take the glass, then when Clare sank into one of the armchairs, making ineffectual fanning motions with one hand, and Delia seated herself on the couch, he went to the other armchair. There was a brief, uncomfortable silence in which the only sound was the tinkling of ice in their glasses.

Then Clare, smiling brightly, asked, "What's your sign, Mr. Flagg?"

He lowered his glass, frowning. "My . . . sign?"

"I'm a Leo. A child of the sun. Slow to anger, but even slower to forgive. What's your birth date?"

"June fifth."

"Gemini. The sign of duality. But Leos and Geminis are usually attuned. Or is that Leos and Aries?" She frowned over that, then with a negligent shrug, "My birthday is July twenty-sixth. I'll be . . ." A short laugh that was almost a giggle. "Well, that would be telling. July twenty-sixth is our anniversary, too. A summer wedding. It seemed like *everything* was in bloom—the wild roses and lilacs. Oh, I hope Lee doesn't forget this year. . . ."

Conan was startled, wondering if he had heard her correctly, and Delia took a deep breath, then reached out for Clare's hand. "Lee *can't* remember, Clare. You know that."

"What?" Two lines between her eyebrows deepened as she looked at Delia, then her chin came up and she laughed. "Don't worry about Lee. He'll come back. He always has."

"No, he won't come back." Delia's tone was still gentle. "Lee is . . . he's passed on, Clare. You remember, don't you?"

Clare hesitated, then replied with a hint of petulance, "Of course, I remember. I just meant . . . well, it doesn't matter."

"Are you going out? I'm glad you put on your hat. The sun can be so bad up here in the mountains."

"I thought I'd find some dandelion greens. I saw some yesterday on Florida." She rose and put her glass on the tray. "And there was some miner's lettuce down on Jordan Creek below the cemetery. My basket—where *did* I put my basket?"

"You probably left it in the kitchen, dear."

"Oh, yes. Well, it was so nice to meet you, Mr. Flagg. Are you staying for supper?"

For a moment Conan was at a loss, then he managed a smile. "Yes, I'll be staying for supper."

"How nice. Well, I must be going."

Delia called after her, "Don't stay too late. Do you have your watch?" But Clare was already out the door. Delia sighed and looked at Conan. Finally, as if she were answering a question, she said, "Clare's always been a little flighty and vague, but when Lee ran off—I mean, when it *seemed* like he'd run off with Amanda Count, I think it was too much for her. She's never been the same."

Conan sipped at his tea, black and sweet, and he didn't find it difficult to imagine Clare in the wake of that disaster. It seemed to cling to her, an unseen shadow, even now. "She was very much in love with Lee, apparently."

"Yes, from the moment they met. She was only nineteen. They were married that same year."

"Was her love reciprocated?"

Delia hesitated, then shook her head. "No. Oh, at first they were regular lovebirds, but Lee always had a wandering eye, and the older he got, the more it wandered. Poor Clare, she always blamed herself for that, because she couldn't have children. She thought she'd failed Lee. Lord, the misery people put themselves through."

"Do you have a picture of Lee?"

She nodded, then crossed to the bookshelves. Conan followed her, waiting as she picked out one of the albums, an old one bound in embossed leather. She turned a few pages, then, "Here. That's Clare and Lee at their wedding."

Conan studied the faded sepia print, and at first his attention was fixed entirely on Clare, as lovely as a princess should be in a lace-veiled gown, yet sweetly vulnerable, a combination against which few men would be proof. Her new husband didn't seem to be, at least not then. His proud smile was that of a man who had achieved ultimate happiness. Yet was there something to be read in the dark, hooded eyes that hinted of future moral failure? Probably not, viewed objectively. All Conan could read in this image, objectively, was that Leland Langtry had been at least ten years older than his bride and stood a head taller, his hair was dark and curly, his face undeniably handsome, and there was power in his wide shoulders and big hands.

Delia said with a sigh, "Lee was a charmer, I'll give him that." Then she put the album away and turned to one of the photographs on the shelf, reaching out to wipe nonexistent dust off the frame. "This is Tom. It was taken in forty-nine, the last proper portrait he ever submitted to."

Tom Starbuck's reluctance to face the camera was evident in the tight set of his mouth, but he seemed to be trying to make the best of it. His was a bony face that age made distinguished; his hair was light, perhaps gray, his eyes webbed in deep lines. On Starbuck, it seemed appropriate to call them laugh lines rather than crow's feet.

There was another photograph next to Starbuck's: a boy about ten years old with one arm around a large dog of indeterminate breed. At the bottom of the picture were the words, "Howie and Baron—1941." Conan didn't ask about that one, and Delia turned to the rolltop desk and opened one of the drawers, the tense resolve in her mouth reminding Conan of the portrait of her husband.

"Here's something you should see," she said.

The object she handed him was a hunting knife. The blade, pocked with rust, was six inches long and an inch wide at the guard. The haft was of elk horn, and on one side was a small metal plate engraved with the initials T.S.

Conan looked at Delia and she said, "Yes, that's the murder weapon. Sheriff Newbolt gave it to me after the inquest. It was Tom's, and he thought I should have it."

Conan nodded and returned the knife to her. "What can you tell me about it?"

She put it in the drawer and closed it. "Tom's father gave it to him when he was a boy. It had sentimental value for him, that's all; Tom wasn't a hunter. Conan, he used it for a letter opener, and he always kept it on his desk at the Lang-Star office. That's something the sheriff and the coroner's jury just seemed to ignore. That knife had been on his desk in plain sight for years. Anybody who walked into his office could've taken it or used it."

"To kill Lee, you mean?"

"Yes."

"Delia, I only have an outline of the story. I'll talk to the sheriff, but I'd like to hear your side first."

She smiled wryly. "Well, Andy Newbolt and I aren't squared off so there's really any *sides* to this thing. It's just that I can't agree with the way he added things up. Why don't we take a walk? I can show you around Silver while I tell you the story—the way *I* added it up."

CHAPTER 3

Delia left the front door unlocked, and Conan smiled at that. He hoped the time would never come when sightseers flocked to Silver City in such numbers that she would have to learn to lock her doors against the larcenous or vandalizing minority.

She paused on the top step of the porch, shielding her eyes against the westering sun. "That's Florida Mountain," she said, pointing to the mountain that loomed in the northwest. Its gentle slopes, gray-green with sage and chaparral between dark swaths of fir and bright green aspen, were broken by gigantic granite mounts and dotted with tailings. "And over there is Potosi Peak," she continued, indicating a slightly less imposing mountain to the southwest. "War Eagle's behind us, of course."

"Asa Starbuck picked a prime lot for the view."

"So he did, but I suspect it was just so he could keep an eye on what everybody else in town was up to."

They walked past the crab apples and down the rocky slope that passed as a road. Finally, Delia began: "About the murder—Lord, I keep thinking of it as the *robbery* still. Anyway, it happened on the night of September twenty-second. Lee was leaving on a business trip to Seattle the next day. He handled the selling and dealing end of the business; he was good with people. Tom tended to the mines and mill.''

"So, this planned trip wasn't unusual?"

"No, but what Lee had planned for it was. The next day was payday at the mill, so there was a lot of cash in the safe: about ten thousand dollars, which was a small fortune in those days. Lee decided to make it payday for himself.''

Conan paused to choose his words. "There's no doubt that he planned to steal the payroll?''

"No. For one thing, that business trip—it was all a lie. Sheriff Kenny called the people Lee was supposed to see in Seattle, and they weren't expecting him. And that night Lee packed his suitcases and put them in his car—all set for the trip, he said—then told Clare he was going up to the office to make sure the payroll was ready for the next day.'' She snorted derisively. "Lee never had anything to do with that. Dex Adler took care of all the bookkeeping, including the payrolls. Lee had no business there at all that night, except his own. And he drove his car up when it was just a short walk. Besides all that, when Dex went up to the office later that night, he found the front door unlocked and the safe open. And the money gone, of course. Only Lee and Tom had keys to that door or knew the safe combination. Nobody else could've opened either one of them.''

"There were no signs of forced entry?''

"No. The sheriff looked for that.''

The battleship-gray walls of the schoolhouse rose on their right now, a massive block of a building two stories high with a bell cupola perched astride the ridgepole. Conan looked up at the windows with their board shutters, as Delia commented, "That old school is eight years older than I am and in better shape. The Owyhee Cattlemen's Association owns it and keeps it up. They let Lettie Burbage have the second floor for her museum. By the way, Lettie was working for Lang-Star at the time of the murder. She was Tom's secretary. Had been since her husband died in thirty-seven. This is Morning Star Street we're coming to. Over there on the other side of Jordan Creek, that queer looking pile—you see, it's five stories high at the back—well, that's the Idaho Hotel.''

It took a stretch of the imagination to accept that huge agglomeration of board walls and odd pitches of roof as the same building he'd seen from the front on his arrival in Silver. Then he turned, distracted by voices, and saw a man and woman—tourists, obviously—lounging on the schoolhouse porch ignoring two shrieking boys, who were killing each other with invisible six-guns.

''Well, speak of the devil.'' Delia stopped, but not out of any interest in the tourists. From the south along Morning Star Street, a wiry little woman in red slacks and flamboyantly flowered blouse was approaching briskly, a pair of glasses, leashed by a chain around her neck, bouncing against her bosom. ''That's Lettie,'' Delia explained.

If Lettie Burbage seemed younger than Delia at a distance, it was only because her precisely curled hair was so dark, but as she came nearer, that was revealed to be a cosmetic subterfuge. ''Just like a little jaybird,'' Delia said under her breath, and the comparison was apt. Lettie walked with her head thrust forward, arms bent at the elbow, and hands raised as if they were constantly ready for something. Her narrow face was dominated by a sharp nose under which her chin receded steeply.

''Afternoon, Delia.'' She was ten paces away when she made that greeting, and it seemed she might pass them without stopping, but Delia waited confidently, smiling, and when Lettie reached them, she halted and put on her glasses to examine Conan.

Delia asked, ''How are you, Lettie?''

But Lettie had no time for amenities. ''This must be Mr. Flagg.''

''So it is,'' Delia agreed. ''Lettie, I'd like you to meet Conan Flagg. Conan, this is Mrs. Letitia Burbage.''

Lettie's thin eyebrows came up, pushing the lines in her forehead into parallel arches. ''Letitia? Oh, Delia, it's been a long time since I heard that. Well, Mr. Flagg, so you're here to look into Lee's murder?'' She only gave him time to nod; then: ''Good. If you ask me, there's more to it than the sheriff—'' The sound of imitation gunfire distracted her to the school. "Damn brats. Well, I got customers, so I better tend to 'em. But, Mr. Flagg, you come around and see me. There's a thing or two *I* could tell you, that's for sure." And with that, she marched up to the school, a ring of keys jangling in her hand.

Delia smiled at Conan. "I don't doubt she *does* have something to tell. She always did know more about other people's business than they knew themselves. But she's got a good heart, really; never was malicious."

Delia turned left down Morning Star Street in the direction from which Lettie had come. This was the same route Conan had followed when he first arrived, but the viewpoint from a car was very different from that of a pedestrian. On their left the sun etched the eroded walls of a row of small, steep-roofed houses, their boarded windows like blinded eyes. Jordan Creek chattered behind a screen of willows on their right, typical wild willows that seldom topped fifteen feet, whose slender, multitudinous stems and narrow leaves always reminded Conan of bamboo.

"About Lee's payday," Delia resumed, "he didn't plan to enjoy it all by himself."

"Enter the 'other woman'?"

"Oh, yes. Amanda Count. She was eighteen when she came here from Homedale. Took typing and shorthand in high school, and she *was* a pretty little thing. Beautiful red hair nearly down to her waist, great big brown eyes, and quite a figure. Well, Lee took one look at her and hired her on the spot as his secretary. She doubled as office receptionist. One thing led to another, of course, but it was two years before it all came to a head, and with Lee that meant it was really serious. He had plenty of little flings before, but none of them lasted more than a month or so. That's the Masonic Hall there."

Conan was looking up at the building, another well-preserved, two-story structure, but this one had lost all its paint. Only one end of it was visible from this point, but as the street curved to the right and the growth of willows thinned, he saw that the building spanned Jordan Creek like a totally-enclosed covered bridge. He asked, "Was space so much at a premium when that was built?"

Delia laughed. "Yes. Doesn't look like it now with so many buildings gone. Winters got a lot of them. And fire. Whole towns have gone up in smoke around here. Silver's been lucky that way, although it's had its share of fires. That must be Mrs. Bonnet."

They were at the bridge crossing Jordan Creek, a simple affair built of four-by-twelve planks. There was no railing, and the bridge was only a few feet above the shallow, swift-running stream; refracted sunlight made pearl and amber patterns on its rocky bed. The woman Delia remarked was standing on the west bank near the Masonic Hall, and it was on the hall that her camera was focused. Her stylish poplin pants and jacket would be suitable on any city street, and her shoes, with their high wedge heels, looked positively dangerous, especially on the gravelly banks of a mountain stream. Her age was made indeterminate at this distance by shoulder-length blond hair whose color and style obviously did not come naturally, and by owl-lensed sunglasses that obscured her face. She didn't seem to notice Conan and Delia; she was too intent on the viewfinder of her camera.

"California," Delia said by way of explanation as they left the bridge behind.

Conan nodded. "That must be her Cadillac I saw in front of the hotel."

"Probably. She's staying at the hotel. Told Jake she's doing a picture page for the Los Angeles *Times*. The livery stable was over here on this corner, then there were houses for quite a way up Jordan Street."

Conan looked to the left, but all he could see was a vine-tangled depression and a few fragments of wood and rusted metal. The ground further to the south looked as if it had never been turned, much less lain under the foundations of houses. On the right at the corner was a building that might originally have been two, but had merged into one, and across and well away from Jordan Street were the two- and three-story backs of a row of buildings that faced onto the next street. They were put together of aged wood and rusty corrugated metal in what seemed an entirely random fashion.

"Delia, did Clare know about Lee's little flings?"

She nodded. "Most of them, I think, although she usually didn't find out till they'd nearly run their course. Then there'd be a big argument, and sometimes if Lee'd had too much to drink, he'd start hitting her, and finally he'd end up on his knees begging her to forgive him and promising it would never happen again."

Conan frowned, thinking of the wedding picture. "What wouldn't happen again—the little flings or hitting her?"

Delia's short laugh was eloquent of disgust. "Both, I guess, and poor Clare, she always believed him."

"But Amanda Count wasn't just another fling?"

"No. Oh, it might've ended up the same finally, but Amanda was a cut above the others. I think she was smart enough to make *sure* it wasn't just another fling."

"Did Clare know about Amanda?"

They had reached the corner now, and Delia turned north up Jordan Street, her pace slackening as she considered that. Finally, she answered, "No, I'm sure she didn't. She never said a word to me about Amanda, and with the others she always came to me as soon as she found out about them. I think Lee was a little more careful that time, although, Lord knows, everybody else in town knew about it."

Conan paused in the cool shade of two towering poplars growing beside the road. To the east there was a space empty of buildings for half a block, and the land sloped down to Jordan Creek and the Masonic hall. He reached out to touch the convoluted bark of one of the trees, then turned and looked across the street. The lay of the land was upward on that side, and they were approaching an open area occupied by only one frame building and a derrick-like structure at the edge of a gravel-filled concavity. There were buildings on the opposite sides of the streets around the open area, and he wondered if it hadn't once been a town square.

He put the question to Delia, but she shook her head as they continued along the street. "That was full of houses and shops at one time. Fire. Like I said, Silver had its share.

There was a mine adit there, too. The ground under the whole town is like a Swiss cheese with all the tunnels. Anyway, to get back to the murder—before Lee left for the office, he and Clare had an argument. She never did tell me exactly what it was about, but it was a bad one.'' Delia's eyes narrowed coldly. ''After we found out about the robbery and Lee—of course, we just thought he'd run off with Amanda—I was the one who had to tell Clare. She was—well, Lee really did it up brown that time. Her mouth was cut, and her nose had been bleeding—it's a wonder he didn't break it—and one eye was swollen shut. That's how he left her—his wife, whom he promised to love and cherish.''

''I think Lee would've been a very hard man to like.''

''Oh, he wasn't always that way; he changed over the years. Bad times bring out the best or the worst in people, and times were really bad in Silver then. That's the store there.'' She waved toward the false-front building on their right, which sported a wide overhang shading a plank walk and a sign proclaiming it the ''General Store.''

Delia added, ''You'll probably want to talk to Vern and Maggie Roseberry. They own the store, and they've been in Silver since twenty-eight. Ten years ago they bought a place in Homedale, and they spend the winters there, but up till then, they were here year-round.''

''I'll put them on my list—along with Lettie Burbage. And Dex Adler. Is there anyone else here now who was around at the time of the murder?''

''No. Oh—I forgot Reuben Sickle. He's a prospector; works a couple of placer claims up Jordan Creek. Well, it looks like Jake is having a lot of business.'' They were at the corner of the street that formed the northern boundary of the ''square,'' and Delia paused, looking over at the hotel, which faced Jordan Street just north of the junction. Four cars were parked in front of the hotel, and two families of sightseers were taking advantage of the shade of the sagging porch.

Conan asked, ''Is Jake another native son?''

Delia smiled as she turned west along the row of buildings on the right side of the street. ''No, he's from Seattle. An engineer of some sort; had his own company making special navigation machines. Sold them to Boeing.''

Conan laughed, and now he understood why Kulik's accent hadn't quite rung true. "What brought him to Silver?"

"Well, Jake always says he was born a hundred years too late. I guess this is as close as he can get to the good old days. His name is really John, you know; he just likes the sound of Jake. His son is John *junior*. But whatever he calls himself, he's done wonders for the hotel, bless him, and he's the kind of person who'd give you the shirt right off his back. Now, this is Avalanche Avenue. The Owyhee *Avalanche*— that was the first daily newspaper in Idaho—was there in that building on the far corner; the one with the gables. The one this side of it, that was the Knapp drugstore.''

Conan studied the elaborately ornamented little false front appreciatively but made no comment, and after a moment Delia returned to the subject of the murder.

"Clare said Lee left the house about eight-thirty that night, and Dex could back her up on that. He happened to be out on his front porch about that time, and he saw Lee drive up to the mill, then he saw a light go on in the office, so he knew Lee went inside.''

"Did Dex see anyone else?"

"No. He had to—I guess he went inside his house then. About ten o'clock he looked again and saw the light was still on. Lee's car wasn't back at his house, and when Dex walked up to the office, it wasn't there, either. The front door was unlocked, like I said, the safe wide open, and the payroll gone. Well, Dex had heard the gossip about Lee and Amanda, so he went down to Mrs. Sparrow's. She ran a boarding house on Washington Street—that's this next street here— and Amanda was living there. Well, of course, Amanda had packed up and gone. She left a note in her room for Mrs. Sparrow saying she wouldn't be back, with some money to pay what she owed on her rent. So, Dex came to the same conclusion everybody else did, and he hightailed it up to our house and told Tom that Lee had run off with Amanda and stolen the payroll. Another artist. Amateur, probably. You can always tell; the more fancy equipment they have, the worse the pictures.''

Conan smiled at that, eyeing the middle-aged woman sitting on the other side of Washington Street rendering the granite arches of a fallen building in oil. Her folding director's chair had the name ''Betty Potter'' emblazoned on the back, and her canvas board rested on an aluminum easel shaded by a striped umbrella. Delia turned left on this street, but stayed to the east side well away from the painter.

''That's the courthouse,'' she said, nodding toward the arches. ''Not the original one, though; that burned down in eighteen eighty-four.'' She smiled to herself. ''Kind of an interesting story about that fire. Seems there was this horse thief—and some said he was a murderer, too—in the jail in the old courthouse when a Chinaman was brought in on a petty theft charge. Well, there was a lot of prejudice against the Chinese, and the horse thief didn't take to being locked in with one of them, so the fool set fire to his bedding, thinking he'd get the jailer's attention with that so he could complain. Trouble was, the jailer was over town, probably in one of the saloons. The courthouse burned to the ground, and the horse thief and the Chinaman with it.''

Conan had to laugh at that macabre tale. ''Is it true?''

''It probably is, sad to say. Anyway, when Dex told Tom about the robbery and Lee, Tom went up to the office, then he called the sheriff. The police looked for Lee for months, but never found a trace of him. That's understandable now, but they didn't find a trace of Amanda or the money, either. Lee's car showed up in Reno, Nevada, the day after the murder, abandoned, the police said; no suitcases in it or anything.''

Conan frowned. Reno was at least 350 miles away. ''Delia, maybe we're dealing with an outsider, a stranger who stole the ten thousand dollars, killed *both* Lee and Amanda, then escaped in the car.'' There were holes in that theory, he knew, even before Delia began pointing them out.

''No, I don't think so,'' she said, shaking her head. ''A stranger would've been noticed around here—it was a small town, even then—and afterward the sheriff questioned just about everybody in town. The only way a stranger could get into Silver without being noticed is if he came after dark the night of the murder. He'd have to go to the mill at exactly the time Lee was there and had the safe open, and then he'd have to *find* the tunnel where the body was left, and that's not easy even in daylight. Then he'd have to take the boards off the adit—it'd been boarded up for years—nail them back on, then get rid of Amanda somehow, and drive Lee's car to Reno. Now, even if all that was possible—and I think it's stretching things—how would this stranger get to Silver in the first place? On foot?'' She gave that a curt laugh. "It's a long walk to Silver from anywhere. But if he came in a car, what happened to it? I mean, if you figure this stranger escaped in Lee's car, he'd have to leave his own car in Silver, and an abandoned car would certainly be noticed. If you're thinking he might've hitched a ride here with one of the townspeople—and who else would be coming up here that time of night?—that would guarantee somebody knowing he was here.'' Then she waved toward a ruined foundation on the right. "That was the brewery. One time, they had a pipeline running under the street across to a storage vat. The Sommercamp Saloon used to be right over there.''

The street sloped upward past the ruins of the brewery, and Conan was surprised at his breathlessness, but considering that the altitude was nearly seven thousand feet, and he'd come from altitude zero, it was to be expected. On the right as the ground leveled, there was another ruin of fallen stone walls.

"The old Heidelberger store," Delia said. "Over here on the other side, that was a butcher shop, then Hawes's drygoods, and the little one on the end was a barber shop.''

Conan studied the block of three buildings, realizing after a moment that these were the fronts of the haphazard, multiple-storied structures he'd seen from the rear on Jordan Street. The barber shop, seemingly tacked onto the others as an afterthought, was tiny, with a peaked false front, at the apex of which a birdhouse was mounted. "That one's marvelous, Delia. Looks like a dollhouse.''

She smiled. "It's one of my favorites. Over here in this

vacant lot next to it—that was where the Chinese Masonic Hall was.

"I didn't know there *were* Chinese Masons."

"Well, there were enough to build a hall. Used to be a couple of joss houses in Silver, too. That little white house across the street is Lettie Burbage's place."

The house, small and fussily neat, seemed to fit its owner. They walked on to the corner of a cross street that connected Washington with Jordan Street, and Delia paused. On the right beyond the corner was a cluster of three buildings, then Washington faded rapidly as it sloped up to a more distant house, tall and spare, that seemed to be the last lonely outpost of the town. Delia had stopped by a cast-iron fire hydrant with the legend, WILLAMETTE IRON AND STEEL WKS. in high relief on the rim below its domed cap.

Conan laughed. "I'll be damned. That's a Portland company, Delia. They're still in business."

She didn't seem surprised. "I guess they put out a good product. This is left over from when we had a water system. Silver was quite the little city at one time."

Conan studied her wistful expression and asked, "Do you regret it—I mean, what's happened to Silver?"

She looked up at him, head tilted. "Oh, I suppose so. It's hard not to regret seeing things change, getting old—including yourself." Then with a shrug she started down the street toward Jordan. "But that's the way of things."

Conan walked beside her silently, considering the poignant stoicism in that phrase. He didn't pursue it.

"Delia, I'd be happy to accept the premise that the murder isn't the work of a casual stranger, but that still leaves—well, how many people lived in Silver at that time?"

"About a hundred, I guess, but I really don't see how it could've been one of the townspeople."

Conan felt a hint of annoyance at that. If it weren't an outsider or a resident, who was left?

"Why not, Delia?"

"Well, the money, for one thing. Whoever killed Lee must've taken the money, and after the robbery—the murder—nobody moved out of town suddenly or showed up with

any unexplained windfalls of cash. That sort of thing definitely gets noticed in a small town. Besides, you have to look
at the robbery, the way it happened. When I said whoever
killed Lee took the money, I meant whoever took it from
Lee. *He* opened the safe.''

At the corner of Jordan Street Delia turned north, and
Conan realized they had almost completed a loop; a short
distance ahead was the street that would take them back over
the bridge to the other side of Jordan Creek.

Delia continued, ''The reason I don't think it was one of
the townspeople is I can't figure any way he'd know Lee was
going to have that safe open and when. Even if this person
did happen to stumble on Lee at the right time, then decided
to kill him—''

''Excuse me, but did Dex or the sheriff find any evidence
of a struggle in the office?''

She turned right at the bridge street. ''No, they didn't,
which makes you wonder if Lee handed over the money
without putting up a fight, and I find that hard to believe. It's
possible, I suppose.''

''Well, the robber-killer might have threatened Lee with a
gun, or if there was a struggle, it might have taken place
elsewhere.''

''Yes, but there's still the problem of getting the body to
the mine—which wouldn't be so hard for a local, I admit,
since he might know where to find it—but what about
Amanda? And how would the killer get Lee's car to Reno?
Not to speak of *why* he'd take it there. If he drove it there
himself, what would he do for a ride back to Silver—*before*
anybody noticed he was gone?''

On the bridge Conan stopped to look at the Masonic Hall.
The California photographer had departed, he noted. ''All
right, Delia, you've made a convincing case against a passing
stranger *or* a resident. Who do *you* think killed Lee?''

She didn't answer immediately, the lines deepening across
her forehead and around her mouth. Finally, she said, ''I
don't know, Conan. I don't even have any suspicions about
anybody. All I know is Tom didn't do it.''

They resumed their strolling pace around the curve of the

road onto Morning Star Street as Conan asked, "Why is Sheriff Newbolt so convinced Tom did do it?"

"The knife, I guess, was the main reason, and then Tom didn't have an alibi for the time of the murder—I mean, between eight-thirty, when Lee went up to the office, and ten, when Dex found the safe open and his payroll gone. Tom was in the parlor working at his desk all evening, but I couldn't prove that because I was busy in the kitchen the whole while. Andy said Tom could've left the house and I wouldn't have known it, and that's possible. The kitchen doors were closed. I . . . didn't want to wake the kids. But I think what it really comes down to is that Andy and the jury were satisfied to blame Tom because they couldn't see any other answer, and that sewed it up nice and neat, with Tom dead. No loose ends to worry about."

"No loose ends!" Conan looked at her, catching the ironic glint in her eye. "All right, how did Newbolt's scenario run—that Tom saw the light in the office from the parlor, went up there without saying a word to you, found Lee ransacking the safe, and in the proverbial fit of rage, stabbed him with a handy letter opener?"

She nodded. "That's about it."

"By the way, did Tom say anything afterward about the knife being lost?"

"Not that I remember, but that doesn't mean he didn't. We were all in a state then. It wasn't just Lee. The money— it was an awful blow losing that much money right then."

A pair of bluebirds sprang into the air from the willows. Conan watched them flashing like jewels as they turned in the sun and finally sank again out of sight in the foliage. "Delia, how did Tom and Lee get along? Any bad blood between them?"

She raised an eyebrow. "Why? You think maybe Andy's right about Tom killing Lee?"

Conan only smiled at that, clasping his hands behind his back. "You're my client, Delia, and my policy is that the client is always right."

"Even if they're wrong?"

"Well, at least until I have irrefutable evidence that they're wrong, which I certainly don't have in this case."

She studied him intently a moment, then laughed. "Fair enough. Well, Tom and Lee did have disagreements, especially in the last year or so when things were going bad with Lang-Star. Lee wanted to sell out, but there wasn't anybody interested in buying then—not the business as such. Tom said all they could sell was the equipment and lumber for salvage and maybe the claims. In the end that's what it came to— selling for salvage. Tom kept the claims, though, and stayed here to put in the claim work. He prospected a lot of new claims, too, cinnabar and molybdenum along with silver, plus running a placer operation for gold. Kept food on the table. Then just before he died, one of the big mining syndicates came in and decided there were real prospects up here after all. Tom made all those claims pay off then. A little late for him to enjoy it, though, except for the satisfaction of knowing he left me and the children well provided for. After Tom died, Dex helped me invest the money, so now Clare and I don't have to worry. But you were asking about bad blood, and all I can tell you is there's a big difference between bad blood and disagreements."

Conan nodded. "What conclusion did the sheriff reach about the stolen money?"

"Well, Andy figured Tom killed Lee in the heat of the moment, then when he saw what he'd done, he tried to cover his tracks and make it look like Lee and Amanda had taken the money and left town." She looked up at the schoolhouse, where Lettie Burbage was waving from a second-story window. Delia waved back, but didn't pause, and as she turned up the road toward her house, her pace quickened.

"Andy couldn't find any evidence at all that Tom ever had the money," she went on, "mainly because he didn't. So, he decided it was Amanda who drove the car to Reno, and Tom used the money to bribe her into leaving town. I guess that was the only way Andy could explain what happened to the money."

"Or what happened to Amanda?"

"Especially that. Amanda was a question mark all around. Just disappeared into thin air."

Conan was silent for a time, and when they reached the crab apples, he stopped in their shade to look north toward the white mound of tailings that was the only thing left of the Lang-Star Mining Company. At the moment, he was wondering—again—how he'd let himself be talked into investigating a murder forty years old. The victim was a silent skeleton, the accused twenty-five years in his grave, and not a stick was left of the site of the murder. Then he frowned and looked around at Delia, who was watching him, waiting.

"Delia, the sheriff assumed the murder took place in the office? On what basis?"

"Well, because Clare and Dex knew Lee had gone up there at eight-thirty, and at ten the door and safe were still open and the light still on. And that's where the murder weapon was. I mean, before the murder. Anyway, it fitted in with Andy's theory, but I don't think I'd dispute it. The murder *is* tied in with the robbery."

He nodded. "The loose end that bothers me most is Amanda Count. If she witnessed the murder . . . well, Newbolt may be right about the killer buying her silence with the payroll." Then, with an oblique glance at Delia, "The killer who was *not* Tom."

"Thank you," she said dryly. "Maybe Amanda was murdered, too. That would explain why nobody could find her."

"Yes, but there's another possibility: she might have been the killer."

Delia squinted up at the tracery of blossoms above her. "Maybe, but from all I've heard, she was as much in love with Lee as he was with her. Love. Whatever it was. Besides, she didn't weigh more than a hundred and five pounds soaking wet, so how could she carry Lee's body all the way up to that mine? Or even drag him? She'd have been all night at that, and the car was gone by ten o'clock."

"That's assuming she killed him in the office. Maybe he went to the tunnel—or, at least, part of the way—on his own two feet."

"Voluntarily?"

"I doubt that."

"Then how would Amanda force him to go up there? By waving that knife in his face? Lee was a big, strong man, and he didn't mind hitting a woman."

Conan sighed. "All right, so that leaves Amanda a question mark still."

"Just like she's always been." Delia looked westward where the sun was verging toward the saddle between Potosi Peak and Florida Mountain. "Well, I guess it's time for me to be thinking about supper."

The house was cool as old houses know how to be however hot the summer. Conan followed Delia through the dining room, skirting the round oak table in the center, and on into the kitchen, a small room with a good part of its space lost to three doors: one into the dining room, another into the back hall, and another opening onto the veranda. Next to that door there was just enough room for a sink and a narrow drainboard; the adjoining wall was taken up with a refrigerator, cupboards, and a wooden counter scarred with use and years. A table surrounded by four chairs blocked the way between the counter and an old nickel-plated, wood-burning cookstove on the wall by the dining room door. Conan smiled, remembering the stove in the kitchen at the Ten-Mile Ranch that his mother had used—steadfastly refusing more modern alternatives—until she died.

"Oh, dear." Delia shook her head as she surveyed the counter, which was littered with packages of cookies, crackers, and bird seed, a jar of peanut butter, another of wheat germ, and a bowl of wild greens. "Well, Clare has come and gone."

"It looks like she was suddenly very hungry."

Delia laughed and began putting the packages away in a cupboard. "No, this is all for her animals. She has a spot over on Slaughterhouse Gulch—she calls it her grove—where she puts food out every morning and evening for the birds and chipmunks and squirrels. I have a feeling crows and coyotes end up with most of it."

Conan screwed the top on the peanut butter and handed it to her. "Well, crows and coyotes have to eat, too."

"Oh, they do around here—and very well. Summer or winter, she gets the food out no matter what, and she has some of the birds and chipmunks eating out of her hand, literally. Clare's one of those people who understands animals, and they seem to understand her. I always said a rattlesnake wouldn't bite Clare; it'd just wait for somebody else to come along." She closed the cupboard, then went to the sink, dumped the greens into a colander, and ran cold water over them. "You don't have to worry about rattlers around here, by the way."

Conan leaned against the counter, hoping his relief at that wasn't too obvious. "I'm surprised. This looks like prime rattlesnake country."

"You'd think so, but there's never been a rattler sighted in Silver. Maybe it's too cold in the winters. There's plenty of them down in the lower elevations." She turned off the water and reached for an apron on a hook by the stove. "Is this Thursday? Yes. Vern will have fresh fryers for me tomorrow, but tonight I guess it's pot roast."

"That's an inviting prospect. Can I help?"

"Oh, Lord, no. I have my own way of doing things. You just go and relax. Oh—do you like a drink before dinner?"

"Well, it's not a habit of mine. I think I'll pay a visit to Dex Adler."

Delia pursed her lips, then reached into a cupboard and took out a quart mason jar. "Take this over to him. He always likes my peaches."

Conan smiled. "Thanks. Maybe this will put him in a more cooperative mood."

CHAPTER 4

Conan stopped at the north corner of the Starbuck house. Dexter Adler was on the porch of his house, but he wasn't alone. At this distance, Conan could ascertain little about the man with whom Adler was talking except that he was big and rangy, dressed in khaki shirt and pants, boots, and a straw hat, and he was carrying a rifle or shotgun.

The conversation ended, and the stranger departed. He didn't come down the road, as Conan expected, but struck off southward, limping noticeably, and was soon out of sight behind the Starbuck house. Adler retreated into his house, the closing of his door a dull thud in the silence. Conan hefted the jar of peaches and started up the road.

His knock was answered by an impatient "Come in!" from within the house. He did, and found himself in a small living room, comfortably but rudimentarily furnished. Adler was apparently a hunter: a rack on the wall near the fireplace held two Remington rifles. Adler's attire was casual now, in keeping with his surroundings. He was bending over the woodbin, filling it with kindling. When he saw Conan, he straightened, his brows coming down. "Oh. It's you."

At that greeting Conan hesitated, then proffered the jar. "Delia asked me to bring this over to you."

Adler eyed the jar, then crossed the room to take it, put it down on a table by the couch, and returned to the fireplace where he began sweeping the hearth with a short broom. He asked sourly, "What do you want, Mr. Flagg?"

Conan almost answered, "Simple courtesy," but restrained himself. "I want to ask you some questions about Lee Langtry's murder."

Adler doggedly persisted at his task. "All I know about Lee's murder I told to the sheriff."

Conan made no response to that, only waiting silently, until at length Adler put the broom aside and turned to face him.

Then Conan said levelly, "Mr. Adler, Delia Starbuck holds you in high regard, and if that regard is reciprocated, I can expect you to help me, not because I ask it, but because Delia has every right to expect it."

"Right!" Adler drew himself stiffly erect. "You've got no *right* to speak for Delia! A private detective! Where the hell did she dig you up, anyway?"

Conan's dark eyes flashed angrily, but his tone was still level. "Ask Delia. I refuse to waste time trying to convince you of the validity of my credentials."

He turned to go, and his hand was on the door knob when Adler rasped, "What *I* want to know is how much do you charge for your private detecting? How much do you expect to stick Delia for? Answer me that!"

Conan opened the door and stepped out onto the porch.

Adler was right behind him. "Wait a minute, Flagg! I want an answer!"

Conan turned, staring at him incredulously, and Adler blurted, "Whatever she's paying you, I'll *double* it! You think about that. I'll double it just to get you damned well out of Silver and your nose out of our business!"

Hands knotted into fists at his sides, Conan said distinctly, "Mr. Adler, go to hell."

There was a moment of silence as Conan stalked away, then he heard the door slam behind him. By the time he reached the Starbuck house, he could even smile at that. It was either smile or get hopelessly angry.

Then as he started up the porch steps, he came to an abrupt stop. The sound at first seemed an echo of Adler's slamming door, but more distant. It seemed to be coming from a point beyond and north of Adler's house, and it was repeated. Two, three, finally four times. Gunshots.

Conan stood listening for a full minute. A wind scented with sagebrush and fir whispered around him, and the blue of the sky was fading as the sun approached the nadir of the curve between the mountains. Finally, hearing no repetition of the shots, he went into the house.

Delia was at the kitchen counter peeling potatoes and placing them around a slab of beef in an enamel roasting pan. A fire burned in the wood stove, its heat putting a flush in her cheeks. She looked inquiringly at Conan. "That was a short visit."

He laughed wryly. "I'm afraid Mr. Adler and I did not part amicably. He seems to think I'm bilking you."

Delia's mouth went tight as she reached for another potato and attacked it with her paring knife. "Now, that's just silly. I'm almost old enough to be Dex's mother, and here he goes trying to mother *me*."

Conan wasn't entirely satisfied with that explanation, but he didn't comment on it. He changed the subject. "I thought I heard shots a few minutes ago."

"Shots? That's odd. We're a long way from hunting season. Maybe it's just potshotters. People are always going out in the hills around here for target practice on their beer cans, then they leave the cans littering up the place."

He nodded. "Is Clare still out?"

Delia frowned as she checked the pendulum clock by the hall door. "Yes, she is, and it's getting late."

"Has she ever gotten lost?"

"No. Clare knows every hill and valley, every tree and rock for miles around here. She's forgetful about some things, but . . ." Delia stopped, listening intently. A moment later Conan heard it, too: a voice calling her name, and it was a cry for help.

"It's Clare," Delia said, and pushed past Conan into the dining room. As she went out into the hall, he was only a pace behind her, and he reached the sitting room in time to catch Clare when she stumbled in the front door, panting, mouth agape, hair flying wildly. But it was her eyes that struck fear in Conan; there was terror there.

"Delia—oh, Delia . . ." She didn't even seem aware of Conan, but reached out like a child for her sister and fell sobbing into her arms.

And Delia held her as if she were a child, a frightened child, smoothing her hair with one hand. "Clare, what's wrong? What happened?"

"Kill me . . . shh—somebody tried to *kill* m-meee . . ."

Delia frowned. "Now, why would anybody want to—"

"I don't *know*! They—they shot at me. . . . Oh!" With a convulsive movement, she covered her ears with her hands.

"Oh, Clare, I don't think anybody was really shooting at *you*." Delia pulled Clare's hands away from her head and held them in hers. "You didn't see anybody, did you?"

"No, I didn't . . . but I *heard*—I heard shooting and somebody . . . in the willows. Oh, Delia . . ."

She began weeping again, and Delia drew her into her arms, murmuring soothingly, "It's all right, Clare, everything's all right. . . ."

Conan asked, "Clare, where were you when you heard the shots?"

She didn't seem to hear him, and Delia had to repeat the question for her. Finally, Clare answered brokenly, "The grove—I was in my grove. Jenny-wren was there, and Whiskers, and a whole little family of bluebirds, and Grayjay . . . then they all flew away, Delia, and—and I heard . . . *where*! Where did you . . . that voice! There was a voice in the willows, and nobody there!"

Delia closed her eyes wearily, nodding as if to herself, then took Clare firmly by the shoulders and led her down the hall. "You're safe now, Clare, so just put it all out of your mind. Come on, we'll wash your face in cold water and comb you hair. You'll feel so much better. We have company for dinner, you know. I'll need you to help me. . . ." The sound of her voice faded as she took Clare through the door under the stairs and on to the bathroom.

Conan closed the front door, looking out through the lace that curtained the oval of beveled glass. The sun hung poised above the curve of the mountains, but its light had an amber cast.

A voice in the willows. Was that a figment of an imaginative but failing mind? Delia's attitude hinted at that, and it didn't seem to surprise her.

A few minutes later he heard footsteps. Delia stopped at the hall doorway. "She'll be all right in a little while."

Conan nodded. "Does this sort of thing happen often?"

"No, but since Lee's body was found—well, it's been hard for her. All these years she kept waiting for him to come home. Now half of the time she's still waiting; she can't believe he's really dead."

"Delia, I'd like to look at her grove. Can you direct me to it?"

Her eyebrows came up. "Conan, she heard the shots—so did you—but she turned them into . . ."

"Something imaginary?"

"I'm afraid so. And that voice—well, she's heard voices before." Delia paused, studying him, then with a sigh, "I'll take you to the grove, but after dinner; after Clare goes to bed. All right?"

He smiled. "All right."

Dinner was a pleasant hour, with a beautifully prepared meal served at the round oak table in the dining room on white damask with Coleport china, Waterford crystal, and Sheffield silver. Clare had apparently forgotten the shots and the voice in the willows; she was vivacious and animated, assuming the role of gracious hostess and playing it well. A chandelier of Tiffany-shaded lamps cast a warm light on the sparkling table, multiplying itself in reflections in the bay window. Clare's gray eyes caught the lights, and she was, briefly, the beauty she had been so many years, so many heartbreaks ago. She talked of the childhood and youth on the Becket family farm on Reynolds Creek, of parties and balls, of picnics and sleigh rides, and even—to Conan's surprise—of Lee Langtry's courtship, portraying him as a handsome, gallant knight in a white linen suit riding up Reynolds Creek to sweep her off her demure feet. But she didn't touch on the aftermath of that courtship.

After dessert—blueberry cobbler, hot from the wood stove—Conan was sent to the parlor to enjoy a cup of coffee and a cigarette while the sisters washed the dishes. He started a small blaze in the fireplace against the chill of the mountain night, and was immersed in an old book on mining when Delia and Clare came in.

Clare said brightly, "I just popped in to say good night, Mr. Flagg. It's been such a pleasure having you visit us."

He had risen, and it seemed quite natural to make a little bow to her. "The pleasure was entirely mine. I hope you sleep well."

"Thank you. Good night, Delia." They exchanged light kisses and Clare departed. Delia listened for her footsteps on the stairs, then turned to Conan.

"I told her I had to see Dex about some business tonight, and you'd be going along. I didn't want to say anything to remind her of what happened—or what she thinks happened—in the grove. My, that fire feels good. I'd better get a coat on before we go." She stood before the fire, rubbing her hands in its heat, and she seemed abstracted, as if she were considering something she wanted to say.

But it was never said. The words were stopped by the sound of a shrill cry from upstairs.

Conan pounded up the stairs, saw the open door and the light in the north bedroom. Clare was standing just inside the door, one hand pressed to her mouth, the other clutching a kerosene lamp whose shuddering flame cast a glaring light on her face, and again there was terror in her eyes. Conan took the lamp from her shaking hand, just as Delia arrived and enfolded Clare in comforting arms, but Delia's eyes were wide with alarm. "Good Lord, what happened here?"

For Conan it was at first difficult to make sense of the clutter around him. The room was large, crowded not only with furniture—the heavy, ornamented Victorian furniture that crowds the most spacious room—but also with pictures, souvenirs, mirrors, jewelry cases, music boxes, jars and vials of cosmetics and perfumes, mementos, ranging from withered nosegays to birds' feathers, bric-a-brac ranging from fine heirlooms to gaudy, plastic contemporary. It was a moment before he realized that the disarray here was extreme and not simply the product of nearly forty years of occupation by a compulsive collector and saver. Drawers were pulled open, their contents littering the floor, bedclothes thrown back, the closet door was ajar, disclosing a tangle of clothing, shoes, and opened hatboxes with their flowered and feathered finery exposed.

Finally, Conan said, "This room has been searched, Delia."

It was midnight when Delia and Conan left the house, armed with flashlights. It had taken nearly two hours for Delia to get Clare calmed, order restored to her room, and Clare in bed and asleep.

Clare had reported nothing missing, and none of the other rooms had apparently been touched. Delia could shed no light on who might have conducted the search, what its object could be, or why Clare's room had been singled out. All she could be sure of was that the search must have occurred this afternoon while she and Conan were touring the town and Clare was out seeking wild greens.

Delia locked the front door behind her, then flicked on her flashlight and led Conan down the steps into the chill, still, black night. Her pace was slow and careful—the only indication that her night vision and sense of balance were in any way diminished by her years—and there was staunch determination in her ramrod posture. Conan followed a few paces behind the shifting circle of light from her flashlight, walking in his own span of light. There was no moon, and the sky presented a spectacle that stopped his breath: the scintillant plumes of the Milky Way wafted across the fathomless black, and individual stars—myriad was the only word for them— seemed not dots on an even dome, but candescent, pulsing lights existing in depth. In this sky perception approached knowledge.

They walked north, footfalls a soft crunching in the fine gravel, and passed Adler's house, but there was no light within it. At this late hour, there wasn't a light in the entire town, and the darkness effectively obliterated it, as if it did not now, nor had ever existed.

Beyond Adler's house, a rubble-choked gully, then another house, the one that had been Clare and Lee Langtry's. Delia veered a little to the right, passing behind yet another house, then the cover of low scrub on the ground vanished, and she turned east up a rutted road. After she had followed it a short distance, she paused.

"I have to find Clare's path. It should be right . . . yes, here it is. This is Slaughterhouse Gulch we're coming to. There really was a slaughterhouse up there. You can still find cut bones here after a rain."

She left the road and continued north down a gradual slope until at length willows loomed in her flashlight. She scouted along them, then stopped, playing her light on something lying on the ground.

It was a shovel, old and rusted, but caked with fresh dirt. Delia picked it up. "I wonder where this came from."

"I wonder what it was used for," Conan countered.

She didn't answer, but carried the shovel with her as she pushed through the willows into a small open area entirely shielded by the dense foliage. Conan's flashlight picked up a scattering of chaff and crumbs. It the spring, or when heavy rains fell, this glade would be filled with the sound of rushing water; the narrow stream bed, dry and silent now between rock walls, descended in steps of fallen boulders, and it seemed as artfully composed as something that might be found in a Japanese garden.

But the sanctity of this grove had been violated.

The purpose of the shovel was explained. It has been used to turn up the ground all around the grove, even to lever smaller stones back and probe beneath them.

"Oh, for the Lord's sake . . ." The shovel fell from Delia's hand with a thud. "Why would anybody do this?"

Conan didn't answer, but began examining the area with his flashlight, privately cursing the darkness. He found nothing, not a clear track, cigarette stub, burnt match, not a human hair or thread of clothing. Finally, he brushed the dirt from his knees and asked Delia, "What about that shovel? Any idea where it might have come from?"

He couldn't see her face, but her voice was tight and uncertain. "No. It might've come from one of the weekender's houses, or, Lord knows, it could've been lying in some pile of boards for fifty years. Do you . . . I suppose this might be the work of some of those crazy kids who come through here. Hippies, whatever you call them. Lot of them stay up at the campground south of town."

Conan doubted that explanation very much. He didn't read this as vandalism but as a deliberate search. Another one. Apparently Delia doubted it, too. She added with an audible sigh, "I'll have to think of *something* to tell Clare. Bottle hunters. Maybe that's more reasonable. They'll dig up anything to find an antique."

Conan didn't comment. It *was* more reasonable than vandalizing hippies, to be sure, and far more reasonable than a voice in the willows that belonged to someone who wanted something Clare had; wanted it enough to frighten her with threats and gunshots, and enough to take the risk of entering the house to search Clare's room.

What was it?

"It's late, Delia. Let's go back." He picked up the shovel as they left the grove, wondering if he'd ever have an answer to his question, and wondering if Clare knew the answer.

CHAPTER 5

The clock on the kitchen wall chimed eight times.

"Good morning, Conan." Delia, sporting a white, bibbed apron, was sitting at the kitchen table chopping rhubarb. Behind her the sink was piled with big-leaved stalks, and on the stove two kettles boiled steamily, one filled with empty mason jars, the other with rhubarb simmering down into a piquant-scented stew.

"Good morning, Delia. I suppose you and Clare have already breakfasted and finished half your day's work."

She laughed, while the knife clack-clacked on the cutting board. "Well, we're usually up and about as soon as it gets light. Pour yourself some coffee. Pot's on the stove."

He found a mug in the cupboard and crossed to the stove where a big, graniteware pot was warming. The coffee was uncompromisingly black, even its aroma invigorating. While he savored a scalding sip, Delia carried the cutting board to the stove and deftly swept the rhubarb into the kettle. "It's going to rain soon. Look at the way that water's boiling off."

Conan stepped back out of the way by the veranda door. "Do you grow the rhubarb?"

"Yes, but you can find it all over town. The Chinese

brought it in." She added more water to the kettle, then
wiped her hands on her apron. "Well, I'd better fix you some
breakfast."

"There's no hurry about that. I want to go over to Clare's
grove and have a look around in daylight. Where is she, by
the way?"

"Out in the garden."

He looked through the glass on the door. Beyond the veranda was a narrow, picket-fenced yard shaded with apple
trees and lilac bushes, most of it given over to a vegetable
garden, the sprouting rows marked with stakes and strings.
In a gathered skirt of blue chambray and a muslin blouse,
her hair confined by a white scarf tied at the back of her
neck, Clare stood among the rows leaning on a hoe, and she
seemed a figure out of a Millet painting.

"Delia, does Clare know about her grove?"

Delia nodded, glancing out toward the garden. "Yes. I
made an excuse to walk over with her this morning. Usually,
she doesn't like anybody going with her; she says they scare
the animals away. But she seemed happy to have me along
this morning. I think she remembers that something happened there yesterday evening, but she wouldn't talk about
it. Anyway, when she saw how the place had been dug up, I
told her it must've been bottle hunters."

"Did she believe you?"

"Well, she seemed to, and she wasn't too upset about it,
thank the Lord." Delia paused, then, "Conan, I . . . well,
I'd sure feel better if I really understood what happened."

"So would I, Delia. We will. Give it time."

A few minutes later, as he left the house, he was wishing
he could truthfully feel that optimistic about eventually un-
derstanding what had happened to Clare. He walked north
past Adler's house. There was no sign of Adler, but a plume
of smoke rose from the chimney. The morning shadows were
still long, a bracing chill in the air. There was something
unique about morning air in the mountains, a quality derived
perhaps from its clarity and from the scent of wild vegetation
untrammeled by urban effluvium. The slopes that seemed at
first glance barren were in fact verdant with inconspicuous

flora blithely thriving in this high, dry land. Wild geranium, fleabane, and buckwheat tended to blend into the subtle coloring of their background, but Indian paintbrush and scarlet gilia were bright beacons of red, and yellow balsam flowers turned their heads sunward, looking themselves like miniature suns.

He had no trouble finding Clare's grove, and the distance seemed much shorter than it had in the depths of the night. As he approached the thicket of willows, a flock of bluebirds whirred into instant flight, and a pair of crows, augmented by a complement of scrub jays, circled overhead, complaining raucously at the interruption of their repast. Within the grove, chipmunks scurried away into the undergrowth, except for one fat and confident specimen who perched atop a rock to watch Conan, disappearing with an irritable squeak and a flip of its tail only when Conan's examination of the area brought him within a few feet.

Conan worked out from the center of the grove, eyes programmed for detail and anomaly, but he found nothing. That didn't mean there was nothing to find, rather that the loose, gravelly soil and the thick leaf rubbish under the willows—which grew so densely he could barely get a hand between the slender trunks—made it extremely difficult to find anything. At length, he departed with an apology to the birds and beasts for interrupting their breakfast. He had hoped to find a cartridge case—Clare had spoken of the gunshots as if they were close to her, and Conan had judged the shots he had heard to be coming from the vicinity of the grove—but he'd have been happy with even a clear foot track; any evidence at all of the voice in the willows or the violator of the grove.

The beauties of the morning were lost on him as he tramped back to the Starbuck house, absently frowning at the happy little suns of balsam. When he reached the house he went directly to the kitchen, where Delia was clearing the table, all the rhubarb consigned to the kettle.

She asked, "Any luck?"

"No."

"Oh. Well, maybe you're ready for breakfast now. Eggs

and bacon all right? I've got some biscuits up in the warming oven. How do you like your eggs?''

The mere words seemed to awake a ravening appetite; the mountain air, no doubt. ''Over easy, if possible.''

''Oh, almost anything's possible,'' she assured him as she delved into the refrigerator.

Conan went to the back door, attracted by the sound of voices. Clare was standing near the veranda now talking to a man Conan recognized, even if he didn't know his name.

It was the man he'd seen on Dex Adler's porch yesterday.

He was not by any means a young man, but his age was hard to judge. The initial color impression was of dusty khaki—clothing, skin, even his hair, which had once been blond but had faded to a streaked pewter tone. He towered over Clare, whose head just reached his wide, angular shoulders, and he still carried his rifle, but it was cradled on one elbow, his head was respectfully bare, his hat clutched in a big, brown hand. Clare was holding a bouquet of wild flowers, and Conan had no doubt her visitor had brought them.

''Delia, who's that man?''

She looked up from the stove briefly. ''Oh, that's Reub Sickle. The prospector I told you about.''

Clare laughed coquettishly at something the man had said, and he seemed to grin—Conan had only an oblique view of his face—and looked down at the ground, shifting his booted feet self-consciously.

Conan said, ''Tell me more about him.''

''Reub?'' Delia shrugged as she slapped a piece of bacon into a frying pan. ''Well, Reub first came to Silver as a young man about nineteen twenty-five, and he's been here ever since, living out in the mountains prospecting for gold. They say he's done real well for himself over the years, but you'd never know it to look at him. I think he's just a born prospector; it's the finding that's important.''

''Where did he come from?''

''Oh, somewhere back east. I think he grew up in an orphanage, but he ran away before he ever graduated from high school and ended up in Nevada. Learned prospecting from an old man he met there, and I guess the life suited him.

Poor Reub was always so shy it hurt. May have been because of his limp. Don't know what's wrong with his foot, whether he broke it as a kid or was just born that way."

"He seems to get along well with Clare." Conan was still watching them through the door panes.

Delia smiled as she crossed to the refrigerator. "Would you like some orange juice? Well, Reub's been in love with Clare since the day he first saw her back in twenty-seven. Of course, she married Lee that year, and there never was room for anybody else in her heart, but that didn't seem to make any difference to Reub. He knew he didn't really stand a chance with Clare, but she was always kind to him. He never seemed to ask for anything more. In fact, I think it would've scared him silly if she'd started taking him seriously."

Conan smiled at that. "It sounds like a very accommodating relationship. I guess I'd better talk to him. You said he was here at the time of the murder."

Delia sighed. "Yes, I almost forgot. Well, you go ahead. It'll be a few minutes before your breakfast is ready. Clare will introduce you."

When Conan stepped out onto the veranda, both Clare and Reub turned, and Conan had a good look at Reub's face for the first time. It was weathered into a network of lines and burned brown with sun, and against that background his eyes were startling—a clear, bright blue as fresh as the morning sky. For a moment those eyes distracted Conan from another feature of Reub's face that was equally startling: the ugly, white scar that slashed a raw line from the left side of his forehead across the flattened, misaligned bridge of his nose to his right cheek.

As if he were aware of exactly what Conan was seeing, Reub put on his hat and pulled the brim forward so that it shadowed his face. Clare said brightly, "Oh, Mr. Flagg, look what Reub brought me. Forget-me-nots and lupine and globe mallow and this"—she plucked out a flower with a delicate green blossom like a tiny Japanese lantern—"here's meadow rue." And Conan almost expected her to add, *O, you must wear your rue with a difference . . .*

Conan said, "They're beautiful, Clare."

"Aren't they? Oh—you haven't met Reub. Reuben Sickle, this is Mr. Flagg. He's visiting with Delia."

Conan offered a hand, which Reub took reluctantly, his sun-browned features set in tense, suspicious lines.

"Mr. Sickle, I'm glad to meet you. Did Clare tell you why I'm here?"

He replied gruffly, "I know why you're here."

"Yes, everyone in Silver seems to. I'd like to talk to you sometime."

"What about?"

Conan saw Clare's smile fading, her gaze turn fixedly on the flowers in her hand. He said, "About . . . the murder, Mr. Sickle. The murder Tom Starbuck was accused of."

"Why talk to me? I never had nothin' to do with that."

"But you were in Silver at the time. I thought—"

"I got nothin' to say about it!" And with that he stalked away around the front of the house, his left foot turning in at the ankle to give him an obvious limp.

Clare called a belated, "Reub? Don't . . . oh, dear."

"I'm sorry, Clare," Conan began, "I didn't mean—"

"Why did you do that?" She looked at him accusingly, her hands in fists, the flowers trembling. "Why do you have to . . . oh, I don't like this! I don't *like* this! Raking over the coals of the past. It's all for nothing!" She turned and started for the kitchen, then abruptly spun about, the tendons in her neck taut as she declared, "It's all a stupid mistake! They say that—that skeleton is Lee. How do they know that? How? *I* know Lee! He'll be back. When he gets tired of that Amanda Count! It's *her* fault, all of it! *Her* fault—that red-haired *bitch*!"

That word on Clare's lips was stunning, and Conan stood silent as she turned and pushed past Delia, who had come to the kitchen door, and on into the house. The flowers were left scattered on the planked floor of the porch.

Conan picked them up and handed them to Delia as he went into the kitchen. "Well, I seem to be off to a bad start today. I hope I have better luck with the sheriff."

Delia mustered a smile and took the flowers. "Better get

these in water. I'm sorry about . . . well, don't take what Clare says to heart.''

''I don't.''

''Good. I'll fix your eggs now. What's this about the sheriff?''

Conan found his mug and poured himself more coffee. ''I think it's high time I had a talk with him. I'm driving down to Murphy after breakfast.''

Delia walked with him to his car, and when they reached the crab apples, Conan looked back toward Adler's house and wasn't surprised to see him standing, vigilant, on his porch.

Delia eyed the high, tenuous clouds moving in from the west. ''Yes, it's going to rain. That'll cool it down a bit.''

Conan nodded, thinking that if it rained he'd have to get the top up on the car. He reached down to open the door, then stumbled back with a hoarse shout.

It was a sound whose terror he'd learned in childhood: the shivering, penetrating rattle that once heard, imprinted itself in the depths of memory as the music of nightmares.

Rattlesnake.

He felt choked and nauseated, incapable of answering Delia's questions. He only managed, when she leaned forward to look into the car, a warning ''Watch out, Delia!''

''It *can't* be. . . .'' The dread rattling never stopped. She jerked back with a whispered, ''Good Lord!'' then ran toward the house, shouting to Conan, ''Don't let it get away!''

He didn't ask how she expected him to prevent that if the snake chose to depart. He mustered the courage to take a step forward and look over the car door. The rattler coiled in thick, shifting loops on the driver's seat, its lethally beautiful head raised, mouth gaping, topaz eyes fixed and certain, it seemed, on him.

''All right, get ready.'' Delia returned, armed with a long-handled shovel. ''When I give the word, you open the door.''

Conan stared at her, then, remembering to close his mouth, nodded and poised himself with a hand near the door.

''Now!''

He jerked the door open, and Delia thrust the shovel in;

the rattle buzzed frantically, and the fanged head whipped forward. She swept the snake out onto the ground where it fell lashing and writhing, but she didn't give it a chance to coil again. The shovel arced over her head and came down with a crunching thud. Twice more it smashed down, and finally the rattling stopped, the beast lay broken and silent, imbued now with a sad, savage innocence.

Delia leaned on the shovel, her breath coming fast, and Conan managed an uncertain laugh. "Delia, I thought you said there were no rattlers in Silver."

"Never were before." She turned at the sound of pounding footsteps. Dexter Adler was running toward them.

"Delia, what happened? What's going on . . . ?" Adler came to a halt a few paces away, staring at the snake. "Oh, my God! Delia, you . . . you didn't kill that thing?"

"Well, it wasn't the first one I killed, Dex. Had the things all over the place down on my folks' farm." She glanced anxiously toward the house. "Better get it buried before Clare sees it. That *would* put her in a state."

Adler reached for the shovel. "I'll take care of it." He glared at Conan. "You had to kill the damn thing, Delia, and that was taking an awful chance. If I'd known—"

"Dex, if I'd waited till you got here, it'd still be rattling. Now, if you want to finish it, fine. I'd appreciate it." And clearly she would also appreciate no further discussion of the matter.

Adler started to say something, then thought better of it, scooped up the dead snake, and carried it across the road in search of softer ground. Conan said to Delia, "Thanks for being so fast with a shovel."

She shrugged that off. "I guess this is one for the books: the first rattler sighted in Silver. Must be the heat brought it out."

Conan didn't challenge that aloud, but as he drove away, he was giving that historic first serious thought. Perhaps the heat did have some bearing on the snake's appearance in Silver, but it seemed too coincidental that it decided to take shelter in his car. For one thing, it would be virtually impossible for the snake to climb up the smooth sides of the car and into the seat. On the other hand, the car made a good temporary cage if it were placed there purposely.

Someone, other than Clare, objected to Conan's raking over the coals of the past. It was a scare tactic, probably, and not designed to be fatal. Snake bites were inevitably painful and debilitating, but with the antivenom serums available now, seldom fatal.

He had to admit the success of the ploy in scaring him, but he didn't even fleetingly consider leaving Silver City or the case. Not now. Rather, he took hope from the ploy. Someone was afraid he might discover something, and that meant there was something to discover. Was it the same someone who had frightened Clare? And what had that someone hoped to find in Clare's room or at her grove?

Perhaps he had learned something about the someone: it was a person with the daring to handle a live rattlesnake, as well as the opportunity and skill to find and capture it.

CHAPTER 6

Conan discovered that he had been in error about Murphy. The entire town was *not* on the west side of the highway: there was an asphalted landing strip on the east side. Murphy was well along in years, its few houses and numerous mobile homes tucked among stately elms and locust trees. He made a tour of the town, which took only a few minutes since he didn't leave his car to look inside the old building—once a school or church—marked ''Library,'' or the modern structure housing the county historical museum, or even the deserted railroad depot, which bore the enigmatic sign, ''Stella's.'' There was only one business, a combination café, tavern, and Conoco station called the Wagon Wheel.

Conan wondered how Murphy held onto the county seat. The majority of the county's residents lived and worked in the towns of Homedale and Marsing in the extreme northwest corner. Perhaps it was simply a matter of location. Murphy was as central as any town in this sprawling county.

But however its presence here was explained, the Owyhee County Courthouse was a proud little building, its meticulously tended grounds bordered by a chain link fence and shaded by venerable trees. It was typical of public architecture of the thirties, spare and trim, with buff brick walls and white marble carved in flat pseudoclassical designs decorating the entrance.

Conan parked by the fence and walked to the gate where a lone parking meter stood. No doubt there was a story behind that. The gate squeaked as he opened and closed it, a comfortable sound in the rural quiet, which was unbroken except for the occasional shrieking rumble of a truck on the highway. A wind had come up from the southwest, moving the leaves of the trees lazily. He passed through a glass door into an interior that was unexpectedly modern in decor, found a directory, then walked down a hall carpeted in moss green toward the back of the building. On the walls hung the earnest efforts of local artists.

In the sheriff's offices, the dispatcher seemed to be the only receptionist, and he was occupied with a radio conversation concerning missing cattle near Bruneau Canyon. Conan waited at the high counter until, the dialogue concluded, the dispatcher turned, smiled pleasantly, and asked his needs and name. The name apparently rang a bell, and Conan was ushered into an office behind a door marked "County Sheriff," and in smaller letters under that, "Andrew Newbolt."

Unlike Delia Starbuck, Andrew Newbolt did not fit Conan's preconception. He seemed at first glance hardly old enough to have graduated from college, although a closer look revealed him to be in his middle thirties. There was an ingenuousness about his freckled, bony face and unruly red hair, but his blue eyes were cool and quick, and when he rose from behind his desk to shake hands with Conan, he moved with the lean proficiency of a cat.

"Morning, Mr. Flagg. Delia said you might be stoppin' by one of these days. Have a chair."

Conan sat down and lit a cigarette, while Newbolt pushed an ashtray over to him, then began deftly rolling a cigarette for himself. Conan said, "If Delia's paved the way, I guess I won't have to explain why I'm here."

But he did have to go through an oblique interrogation in the guise of small talk designed to reveal his qualifications and intentions. Conan volunteered his investigator's license, touched casually on his training in G-2, on other cases he'd been involved with, and dropped a few names, such as Steve Travers, Chief of Detectives for the Salem Division of the Oregon State Police.

The latter was well chosen. Newbolt nodded. "I heard about Travers. Come from Pendleton, didn't he?"

"A ranch near Pendleton, yes. We grew up on neighboring ranches."

"Delia says you had something to do with the Ten-Mile."

"I still do. When my father died I incorporated the ranch. I'm majority stockholder." Then to forestall Newbolt's next question, he added, "I decided there were other people far better qualified to run the ranch than I. Business isn't my forte."

"So, you went into private investigating?"

"Among other things."

Newbolt didn't pursue that, apparently taking the hint in Conan's flat tone. "Well, Mr. Flagg, I don't envy you one bit on this Langtry thing. Maybe you'll have better luck on it than I did. Far as I'm concerned—and the county—the case is closed."

Conan took a slow drag on his cigarette. "Have you any objections to Delia reopening it—unofficially?"

"Nope. That don't mean I think it's a good idea or that anything'll come of it, but I like Delia. Known her since I was a kid. I knew Tom, too."

"Well enough to judge whether he was capable of murder?"

Newbolt's eyes narrowed. "I'm not in the judgin' end of things." Then he rose and went to a file cabinet, and after a brief search, returned with three folders. "The big one's the file on the murder. The others date back to nineteen-forty: the robbery report and the missing persons reports on Langtry and Amanda Count."

Conan opened the last one first, but it contained only a history of the fruitless search for Amanda Count and the known facts of her life: date and place of birth, names and addresses of relatives and friends, occupation, last known address, physical description. Height, 5 feet, 3 inches;

weight, 107 pounds; eyes, brown; hair, red; age, twenty years. There was a photograph, probably a high school graduation picture, and Amanda had definitely been, in Delia's words, "a pretty little thing." There was something haunting in her dark eyes, extraordinarily beautiful eyes, that offered no quarter to the world, and expected none; something haunting in her defiantly confident smile, in her very youth. She would be sixty years old now. *If* she were still alive.

Conan said irritably, "Damn, she's the key to this thing. What *happened* to her?"

Newbolt laughed at that clearly rhetorical question. "I'd give a lot to know that myself, but there was no way I could look for her properly after Langtry's body showed up. I've got four deputies and a county big as New Hampshire, Vermont, and Rhode Island put together to tend to. Only about six thousand people, but just gettin' around in it takes time."

"And I doubt any other law enforcement agencies were interested in looking for Amanda after forty years. What do you know about her—I mean, other than what's in this file?"

Newbolt stretched out, tipping his chair back. "All her folks are dead or gone now, except a sister. Doris Lea. Accordin' to her, they had a rough time growin' up. Dirt poor, and their father was a bum and a drunk. Got his kicks beatin' up on his wife and kids. There was five kids altogether. Doris was the oldest, and Amanda was next by a year. Anyhow, Amanda had looks and brains, and she didn't plan on livin' poor and hard the rest of her life."

"That's from the sister?"

"Nearly everything I got is from the sister. She was the only one in the family Amanda gave a damn about, or gave a damn about Amanda. So she says, anyhow."

"Could the sister tell you how Amanda really felt about Lee Langtry?"

"Well, Doris said it was nothin' less than true love for Amanda, even if he *was* old enough to be her father. Maybe that's what she was lookin' for. I guess her old man had a nickname: 'No-count' Count."

"There's no doubt in Doris's mind that Amanda planned to run away with Lee?"

Newbolt shook his head, puffing out a pungent cloud of smoke. "No, not in Doris's mind."

"Did she have any ideas about what happened to Amanda after the murder?"

"Well, she thinks Amanda was *alive* right afterward. Told me she had a post card from her. Came a few days after Amanda and Langtry disappeared, postmarked Reno, Nevada."

Conan leaned forward at that, but nothing in Newbolt's attitude suggested he should take hope from it.

"Sheriff, what did Amanda say in the card?"

"Just that she was all right, and Doris wasn't to worry about her, but they'd probably never see each other again. The trouble with that card, though, is Doris didn't show it to anybody back when she got it. Figured Amanda was in trouble, what with the robbery and all, and Doris didn't want to point the police in her direction. After that . . . well, she lost the damn thing. All we got is her word for it, and the poor old gal is in a nursing home in Boise now and not too clear in the head. So, maybe there really was a post card, and maybe there wasn't. No way to be sure."

Conan sagged back in his chair. "Lee's car was found in Reno, wasn't it?"

"Right. Locked and empty. No luggage, no nothing."

"Fingerprints? Any indication of foul play?"

"If the Reno police checked for that, they didn't keep any record of it."

Conan frowned, wondering—yet again—why he'd been so foolish as to take a case this old. Curiosity and Delia Starbuck. And what kept him on it? Curiosity and a rattlesnake. He opened the file on the murder, finding that most of the information only added detail to what he already knew from Delia. "There was no doubt about the identification of the body, Sheriff?"

"No way. First, we had dental records. Langtry's dentist—fella from Homedale—is still around and kept good records. Besides—" His chair squealed as he tipped forward to reach across the desk. "—take a look at the pictures. You can see there *was* still something left of the clothes and—that next picture, his wallet.''

The wallet had been opened to show a faded, water-spotted driver's license. Conan nodded. ''Was there any money in the wallet?''

''Yes. Wasn't in very good shape; hard to count. There was at least a couple hundred bucks, though.''

Conan raised an eyebrow, but didn't comment on that as he leafed through the photographs of the body as it had been found in the mine adit. In the harsh strobe light, it seemed alien and unnatural in its rocky tomb. The knife stood stark against the rotting fragments of clothing.

He asked, ''There was no question about the cause of death?''

Newbolt laughed curtly. ''Well, he could've been poisoned, too, but it'd have to be a damn fast-acting to get him before that knife. No cranial trauma or unhealed breaks in the bones except where the knife went in. Scraped the ribs and cracked one. Whoever used it wasn't kiddin' around.''

'' 'Whoever'?'' Conan gave Newbolt a slanted smile.

He reciprocated the smile as he stubbed out his cigarette. '' 'Whoever' had to be a big, strong man—or a damned Amazon. Somebody like Tom Starbuck. He stood about six foot.''

-*''Touché,''* Conan replied, turning to a list of personal effects. ''Was there anything missing from the body?''

''Well, a couple of items—*maybe*. His wedding ring and a gold pocket watch. Clare gave him the watch on their first wedding anniversary. She said he had both of 'em with him when he left the house the night he was murdered. Of course, Clare gets a bit . . . confused. Anyhow, they weren't on the body.'' Then he shrugged, linking his hands behind his neck. ''Pack rats could've got 'em. They like shiny things like that, and there was rats around. Some of the bones had tooth marks.''

Conan studied the pictures of the body. ''Pack rats might explain the missing watch, but not the ring. Look at his left hand. The fingers are curled under against the ground.

There's no way a pack rat could get a ring off his finger without altering the position of those bones.''

Newbolt reached for the photograph and frowned at it, but he didn't seem particularly concerned about Conan's observation. "Well, Mr. Flagg, I'll grant you that. Who knows, maybe Tom took the ring and watch after he killed Langtry.''

"Why? They'd be highly incriminating if they were found." He paused, then, "Of course, we can't be sure Lee had them with him. Yes, I'm well aware of how 'confused' Clare can get. But we *can* be sure the knife was left in the body. If Tom killed Lee, why would he leave something as incriminating as that knife?''

"I can't answer that. Wish to hell I could. It was wedged in damned hard, though. Maybe he couldn't pull it out. Anyway, we're not talkin' about a premeditated murder here. I don't figure Tom was thinkin' too clear after he killed Langtry.''

Conan let that ride. He leafed through the file again, then closed it. "What about the actual site of the murder? The office?''

"Well, probably. Lights were still on, the door open, and so was the safe when Dex Adler got up there about ten, and Dex saw Langtry go into the office at eight-thirty. But there's no solid evidence. It could've happened somewhere else, I guess, but it don't seem likely.''

Nor did it contribute to the case against Tom Starbuck, Conan added to himself. He asked, "There was no sign of a struggle in the office?''

"Not accordin' to the reports Sheriff Kenny made on the robbery in nineteen-forty." The jangle of his phone brought him suddenly upright; he snatched up the receiver. "Newbolt." A series of affirmative grunts and unconscious nods, then, "Right. The 'copter's over to Riddle right now. I'll radio Danny to meet you at Three Creek. I'll get there soon as I can." He rose as he hung up. "Sorry, Mr. Flagg, but I've got to go. Light plane crashed down on the Jarbidge River.''

Conan was already on his feet. "Thanks for your time, Sheriff, and the information.''

Newbolt rounded his desk and picked his Stetson off a hat rack. "You're welcome to the information. Hope it helps."

"So do I, Sheriff. So do I."

CHAPTER 7

Before leaving Murphy, Conan stopped at the Wagon Wheel for gas and coffee, staying for a second cup while he eavesdropped on two sun-hardened, Levied buckaroos discussing the local rodeo circuit. On the drive back to Silver City, he still had the top down on the car, but the sun's heat was tempered with a curdling of cloud, and ominous thunderheads were mounting beyond the Owyhees.

But the sun was still shining, if intermittently, in Silver, and John Kulik's friends were still hammering at the upstairs railing of the Idaho Hotel's porch. They waved as Conan passed. Mrs. Bonnet was still taking photographs—her subject, the store—and the artist, Betty Potter, was still painting—her subject, the Masonic Hall. And all's right with the world, Conan thought wryly as he parked under the crab apples.

He put the top up on the car, then went into the house, where he was greeted with the heady aroma of lunch in the making. It was served on the kitchen table: thick, savory vegetable soup—"just something to do with the leftovers," Delia insisted—slabs of homemade bread, and cherry pie hot from the oven. Conan was beginning to think he had at least come to a *gastronomic* Shangri-la. Clare was in good spirits, her outburst of this morning apparently forgotten, and when she mentioned that she had to go to the store and Conan offered to accompany her, she acquiesced willingly.

As they descended the porch steps, she looked up at the sky. "Yes, it's going to rain; you can feel it. That'll be good for the asparagus."

"I gather you're the gardener of the house."

"Oh, I like to grow things, and they seem to like growing for me." She stopped at the side of the road, then picked something up from under a sagebrush. "Part of some Chinaman's rice dish, I'll bet." She handed her find to Conan, a shard of white pottery with a leaf design glazed in blue and unmistakably Chinese in style. "You can keep it."

"Thank you, Clare. It'll be a good memento of Silver."

For a while she walked in silence, eyes turned down on the road, then she said, "I love the way the mica glitters. In Silver I'm always walking on stars. Do you believe in reincarnation, Mr. Flagg?"

That stopped him for a moment. "Well, I think it's an intriguing concept."

They had reached the front of the schoolhouse, and Conan saw an American flag thrust from an upstairs window; Lettie Burbage's museum was apparently open for business. As Clare turned left onto Morning Star Street, she said matter-of-factly, "I'm coming back as a bluebird. Or perhaps a tree. A mountain mahogany. They're so small and dainty, but, oh, they're strong. Or a fir tree; one of those tall, slim ones, like church spires. God speaks best through the trees, you know."

She looked at Conan expectantly, and he commented, "They're certainly one of God's finest expressions."

"They're old souls. Now, Lee , , ," She gazed up into the blue-and-white mottled sky. "He'll come back as an eagle; a golden eagle flying high over the mountains. . . ."

Conan could muster no response at all to that, but he didn't have to. They were near the Masonic Hall, and Clare left the road and crossed a grassy clearing toward Jordan Creek. "This is a short cut. Water's not too high now, but you have to watch out or you'll get your feet all wet."

Conan let her lead the way, smiling in amazement as she stepped agilely from one rock to another, the icy water chattering within inches of her feet. When she reached the bank, she turned, laughing. "I've never fallen in yet!"

Conan was waving his arms for balance. "I hope you can keep that record intact." Then as they walked up the slope behind the store building, he asked cautiously, "Clare, do you remember a gold watch you gave Lee?"

"Of course. It was so beautiful. It had a—what is it called? Greek key. Yes, a Greek key design on the back. I gave it to him on our first anniversary. I said all our anniversaries would be golden." And her bemused smile gave no hint that they weren't.

"What happened to that watch?"

"Oh, Lee still has it. He always wore it."

There was at least a discrepancy in tenses there. "It wasn't among his personal effects, Clare. Did he have it with him the night he was killed?"

She walked on, putting her back to him. "Why do you have to keep asking questions? I don't want you to keep asking *questions*!"

Conan followed her up a steep path toward the street; the walls of the store and hotel loomed above them on either side, reminding him of battered Louise Nevelson bas-reliefs. He said, "All right, Clare, we won't talk about it now." She didn't respond to that, but the tense set of her shoulders relaxed. In the open space between buildings stood a vault walled in stone, with an elaborately decorated iron door. Conan asked, "Was there a bank here?"

She turned. "Oh, that was in the Wells Fargo office. It was still standing till about thirty years ago."

This brought them to Jordan Street, and Clare stepped up onto the plank walk fronting the store and peered in the windows, but their reflections revealed more of the exterior world than of the dim interior. "Let's see, what *did* I do with that list?" She found it in a pocket, and started to open the door, but it swung away from her, the handle jerking out of her hand. She gave a startled, "Oh!"

The person who had inadvertently snatched the door from her stood equally startled just inside the store. Mrs. Bonnet, her dark glasses poised in one hand. At close range and without the glasses, her face showed her to be well past her youth, but clearly affluent and concerned enough to make it impossible to determine how far past. Nor had she relinquished her figure to years; she would still fit nicely into a size ten. After the initial surprise, she smiled and hurriedly put on her glasses, covering brown eyes that Conan noted as her best feature.

"So sorry," she murmured, slipping past Clare, "I wasn't watching where I was going." She gave Conan a brief scrutiny, then hurried off toward the hotel.

Clare watched her, frowning slightly, then when Conan opened the door for her, started into the store again. Then abruptly she stopped, staring straight ahead, her mouth open, moving soundlessly. A moment later, she careened into Conan and ran out the door, footfalls thumping on the planks.

He stared blankly after her. "Clare?"

But she had disappeared around the corner of the store. He frowned irritably, then followed her, pausing just beyond the corner where he could see her stumbling down the slope toward Jordan Creek. "Clare! What in—*Clare!*"

She didn't look back or stop, but broke into a halting run, and Conan, remembering her age with dread visions of heart attacks and strokes, ran after her, watching with a sinking sensation as she negotiated the creek. She didn't fall, although she was wet to the knees before she reached the other side. The frigid water didn't stop her, nor did Conan's shouts, and he didn't catch up with her until she reached Morning Star Street, and by then he was wondering about his own heart at this altitude. He caught her arms and spun her around.

"Clare, for God's sake, what—"

But she began struggling frantically, small hands flailing at him while she shrieked, "Get *away* from me! I don't know—I don't know where it—let me go! *Let me go!*"

In films, this was the time for a smart slap across the face, but somehow Conan wasn't up to that. He let her go. She darted away, but after half a block, when she reached the schoolhouse, she was forced to pause to catch her breath. Conan waited patiently until she continued up the road to the Starbuck house at a limping, half run, then he followed at a leisurely walk. Lettie Burbage, he noted, was taking all this in from her second-story observation post, but when he looked up at her, anticipating with no relish a barrage of inquiry, she abruptly withdrew.

Voices carried with extraordinary clarity in the mountain air, and well before Conan reached the house, he heard Clare calling Delia, then Delia's questioning responses. And another voice. When he passed the crab apples, Delia was at the foot of the porch steps holding Clare, and Dex Adler was scowling at Conan as he approached.

Adler demanded, "What did you *do* to her?"

"I tried to stop her before she had a heart attack, but apparently her heart is better than I anticipated."

Delia, looking over Clare's head, smiled at that. "Clare, it's all right now. Just calm down. . . ."

Clare turned her tear-reddened face toward Conan. "Somebody tried to kill me again, Mr. Flagg."

Adler exploded, "Oh, damn! Now, this has gone too—"

"No one was trying to kill you, Clare." Conan spoke quietly, but firmly. "I was just trying to stop you before—"

"No! No! I saw—somebody was *chasing* me! Don't treat me like I'm crazy. I'm *not*!"

Delia took her in charge, guiding her toward the steps with an arm around her shoulders, murmuring soothing words. When they had disappeared inside the house, Adler gave Conan a withering look. "No good is going to come of all this." And with that pronouncement, he stalked off toward his house.

Conan sat on the steps and lit a cigarette, at the moment inclined to agree with Adler, and wondering what had triggered Clare's irrational flight. Mrs. Bonnet? Or something she saw—or simply imagined—in the shadowy interior of the store? He was still pondering a quarter of an hour later when Delia joined him on the step.

"She's calmed down now," Delia assured him. "Lord, I don't know what gets into her. What happened?"

Conan told her, but she found no enlightenment in it. "Mrs. Bonnet? I don't think Clare even knows her name. Maybe she reminded her of somebody. Did she have red hair?"

"No, she's blonde." He came to his feet. "I'll get your groceries if you have the list." Then when she brought it out of her apron pocket, "Are you in a hurry for this?"

"Well, I was planning on the chicken for supper."

He smiled. "You'll have it. I just wanted to stop by the schoolhouse while Lettie's there."

CHAPTER 8

It was an elegant building, the schoolhouse, and before he went inside, Conan stopped to contemplate it, noting the refinement of the triangular pediments over the windows, the perfect symmetry of the placement of doors and windows. No doubt the basic plan had been drawn on the golden section.

Within the open door, he paused in a small anteroom, then made his way to the stairs on the left-hand wall, passing an ore cart and an assortment of mining equipment. The walls were crowded with old photographs and maps of mines that bore out Delia's assertion that the entire area was riddled with underground tunnels. Here were feats of engineering as astounding as any Pompeii or Troy could offer.

He heard voices from the second floor, and when he reached the small room at the head of the stairs, saw Lettie Burbage tilted back comfortably in a chair behind a cluttered desk reminiscing with an elderly couple. One wall of the room was jammed with a collection of lavender-tinted glass objects, while a display of Chinese artifacts filled most of the rest of the space. The desk was dominated by a bronze cash register with "Idaho Hotel" cast into the elaborate design.

Conan took the hint and pulled out his billfold, remembering the sign posted downstairs requiring an admission fee of fifty cents.

Lettie broke off her conversation with the visitors. "Afternoon, Mr. Flagg." She leaned forward to take his ten-dollar bill.

"Keep the change," he said, "for the museum."

Lettie beamed and deposited his contribution in the cash register. "You go on in and have a look around. I'll be with you in a little while." Then she resumed her reminiscences as Conan went through the open door into the large room that constituted the museum proper.

Lettie's "little while" turned out to be quite a long while, but Conan didn't object. There was enough here to occupy him for hours. In the center of the room stood a big, round wood stove, a minor masterpiece of Victorian baroque design. Other pieces of furniture were scattered about: school desks, a spinning wheel, a sewing machine patented in 1877, an Edison phonograph with a morning-glory speaker. Mannequins in period costumes looked blankly at him from amid the diverse collection: tools, saddles, harnesses, snowshoes, sleigh bells, cowbells of all sizes; iron and enamel pots and pitchers; a molting stuffed owl; bullion molds two and three feet in length, gold pans and ore buckets; the copper worm from a still; wash tubs, cheese molds, butter presses, churns, sad irons, and a small wood stove with mounts for four irons used in a Chinese laundry; early thermoses and an incredible variety of kerosene lamps; the jewelry, cosmetics, gloves, and purses worn by fashionable ladies, the bone-and-lace fans that cooled them in vanished summers. There was even a small coffin, painted white, with a glassed oval in the lid.

It was a random sampling of the everyday life—even unto death—of another era, and Conan wondered what a similar sampling of his era would be like seen a hundred years hence. He had made the entire circuit of the room and paused now near the door to study what at first appeared to be a wreath of dried flowers mounted behind glass in a deep frame. A closer look and a typewritten sheet posted by the frame disabused him. The flowers were made from "locks of hair

from departed family members," and were commonly hung
in parlors. That, Conan decided, was one aspect of this by-
gone era that was well by-gone.

When at length he heard Lettie's visitors making their
adieus and clumping down the stairs, he returned to the anteroom where Lettie was lighting a cigarette with a wooden
kitchen match.

"Have a seat," she ordered. "What d'you think of it?"

Conan went to the chair by the window and lighted a cigarette for himself, and, on the assumption that she was re-
ferring to the museum, said, "You've done a marvelous job
collecting and displaying all that, Mrs. Burbage."

"Thanks. Course, it wasn't just me got ever'thing together. Call me Lettie. I'll call you Conan. Indian name?"

"No. Irish."

"Oh." Her raised eyebrows furrowed her forehead, but
he didn't elaborate. "Well, Conan, you made any progress?"

"On Lee's murder? I'm not sure yet. Delia told me you
were Tom's secretary."

"Right. From October of thirty-seven after Martin died—
my husband—till September of forty-two when the mill
closed."

"I wonder if you could draw me a rough floor plan of the
office. It helps me to visualize things."

She looked at him as if she thought he was a little mad,
then shuffled through the debris on the desk and found a
piece of paper and a pencil, then caught her leashed glasses
and perched them on the bridge of her nose. "Well, it was a
separate building, but stuck onto the side of the mill. Let's
see . . ." She made a tentative rectangle about twice as long
as it was wide, her pencil moving erratically. "The mill was
back here—" she extended one of the long walls to indicate
the wall of the mill. "—and the front door was in the middle
of this wall." That was the other long wall. "Altogether
there was six rooms like . . . this. See—two rows of three
rooms each. Now, when you first walked in—from the front,
I mean—this was sort of a reception room. That's where
Amanda's desk was. There was a door on each side." She

made agitated marks that no architect would recognize as symbols for doors. "On the left, that went into my office. I had my own. Then there was a door out of my office to Tom's here in the back corner. When you took the right-hand door out of the reception room, that was Lee's office. Then Dex Adler's office was in the other back corner. There was a hall—made a sort of an L—connectin' Dex's and Tom's offices and leadin' to this back door into the mill. This little space left here, that was the foreman's office."

The drawing wasn't a great deal clearer than her explanation, but Conan only nodded. "Tell me about the foreman."

She unhooked her cigarette from her lower lip, where it had hung, defying gravity, throughout her exposition. "Tell you *what* about him? Oh. You're wonderin' if *he* could've had something to do with what happened. Well, I don't figure you have to worry about Will. Will Day, that was his name."

Conan asked patiently, "Why shouldn't I worry about him?"

"Because he wasn't anywhere near Silver when Lee got murdered. Poor Will had a heart attack 'bout a week before. He was down to the hospital in Homedale. Didn't come back to work at the mill for—oh, nearly six months."

And that took care of Will. Conan leaned forward to study the drawing. "Where was the safe?"

"Right here in Tom's office." She penciled in a small square in the corner where the mill wall and the interior wall of the office met. "Tom's desk was kind of in the middle facin' the front of the building. Liked to have his back to a wall. Inter-estin' about that. So'd Lee and Will, but Dex Adler—he had to have his back to the window. Said he didn't like distractions."

The drawing was becoming more muddled with every word, but Conan persevered. "Where were the windows?"

"Oh, there was windows on every outside wall. These front offices—mine and Lee's—had two: one on the front of the building, the other on the side. The back offices just had the one."

He pointed to the wiggly line she had drawn in the exterior

wall of Starbuck's office. "If someone were standing outside this window, could they see into the office?"

"Sure." She puffed on her cigarette, squinting at him through a cloud of smoke. "The ground sloped up at that end. Wouldn't be no trouble at all."

"When did you see the office—I mean, after the murder?"

"The very next mornin'. Course, we just thought it was a robbery." Then she leaned toward Conan. "Ever'body always made out like nothin' was touched in there 'cept the safe, but I can tell you, that wasn't the way it was. I told Sheriff Kenny then, and Andy Newbolt again after they found Lee's body, but neither one of 'em paid any attention. Ol' Lathe Kenny figgered all women was blind and dumb, and Andy—well, he said it all happened so long ago, like maybe my memory was gone."

Conan frowned sympathetically. "How *was* it, then?"

She leaned back, apparently prepared to give the devil its due now that she had a willing listener. "Matter of fact, there wasn't a lot to see. Just little things. Like Tom had one of them appointment calendars on his desk, and it was open to the wrong date, and it was on the *right* side of the desk, when he always kept it on the *left* side. Then I'd put a bunch of letters on his desk for him to sign, and they was all out of order, and there was a pile of maps on the table between the extra chairs by the hall door, and I *knew* I put them on top of the file cabinet the day before."

Conan's eyes narrowed. "Do you think the office might have been searched?"

She gave that some thought, then shook her head. "No, I don't think so. Nothin' in the files was out of order, and the desk drawers—well, after the sheriff finished, I started lookin' for that knife. *I* noticed it was gone right off, but nobody else was interested, least of all poor Tom. He was just plain frantic, it bein' payday and no money for the men. Anyhow, I looked in the desk for the knife, and ever'thing was just like it always was. Tom was neat about his desk, so if anybody'd been riflin' through it, I would've known. No, I don't think anybody searched the place, but I *do* think things got moved around in there. Somethin' else, too." She glanced out the window, as if someone might be clinging to the sill eaves-dropping. "One thing in particular I noticed: there was a little rug by the hall door—least, that's where it *usually* was—but when I come in on the day after the murder, that rug was over in front of Tom's desk. Well, I started to put it back where it belonged, and that's when I saw the stain." She paused for effect.

Conan took his cue. "What kind of stain?"

"Don't know for sure. A big, dark spot. The floor was just oiled boards, y'know, and whatever it was had soaked in. Anyhow, somethin' really queer happened then." Her eyes went to bright, cold slits. "Dex Adler happened to see what I was doin'—Tom wasn't there; out talkin' to the men, I think—and Dex told me to leave the rug alone. Just like that. Never saw him—what is it they say?—so uptight. Said he spilled some ink on the floor and didn't want to bother Tom about it. So, I left the rug where it was. Next day, it was back where it belonged, and the spot had been scrubbed out."

Conan took time for a long drag on his cigarette, then, "Did Adler do the scrubbing?"

She raised an eyebrow and gave Conan an oblique look. "Well, *I* sure didn't, and I don't figger Tom even noticed it. Now that it turns out Lee was stabbed with that knife—the one that was right there on the desk—well, it don't seem very likely to me it was an *ink* stain." Conan waited, and she added portentously, "More like a *blood* stain. And the way things was moved around, well, I think there'd been a fight in that office, and somebody tried to cover it up and put ever'thing back like it was—or like they *thought* it was."

Conan smiled as he crushed out his cigarette in the ash-tray. At least now he could be relatively sure of the site of this murder, even if nothing was left of it except a mound of tailings and Lettie's enigmatic drawing. "Why would Dex be so concerned about that stain?"

She replied archly, "Makes you wonder, don't it, Conan?"

It did indeed. Not only about Dex Adler as a suspect, but why Lettie was so willing to present him as such. Lettie went on, "Dex was a quiet one, but like they say, still waters run

deep. Him and Irene come here, oh, about in thirty-five from
back east somewhere; Illinoys or Indiana. Saved all the
money they could and put it into real estate. Dex was smart;
buy cheap and sell dear, that was his idea, and land was damn
sure cheap back then. Course, you couldn't *sell* it; nobody
had any money. But Dex figgered if he could hold on long
enough, we was bound to pull out of the Depression, then
that land would be worth a fortune. He was right, too. But I
happen to know that in nineteen-forty he run into some real
trouble. Irene got sick, y'know.''

"Delia said she died in forty-two."

"Yes. Poor thing. She got leukemia, and the doctor bills
kept pilin' up. That's how Dex got into trouble. Overex-
tended himself. About a month before the robbery, he got
foreclosure notices on practically all his property.''

"How did you find out about that?"

She eyed him sharply, then shrugged. "Oh, I always had
good ears, and I used 'em. But I didn't use my mouth 'less
there was damn good reason to. Now, the inter-estin' thing
about Dex's money troubles is that right *after* the robbery,
he got *out* of trouble. Then about a year later, he made his
first big sale, and it was easy goin' for him from then on.
Why, that man's a millionaire now. Has himself a big, fancy
house in Boise and his own airplane, yet.''

"But he never remarried?"

"No. Guess he just never got over Irene."

Conan gave that a moment of respectful silence while he
lighted another cigarette, then when Lettie took out a Camel,
he leaned forward to light hers. "Tell me about Lee."

"Oh, my God!" She blew out a puff of smoke, her thin
mouth twitching in disgust. "That man made a martyr out
of poor Clare. He chased after anything in skirts. All a woman
had to do was smile at him, and he'd be off and runnin'. You
can bet your boots he never started after *me*. I never even let
him get to the smilin' stage.''

She put her long nose in the air with that, and Conan
sensed a hint of pique. Lettie had been a relatively young
woman when she went to work at Lang-Star, newly widowed

and no doubt lonely. He wondered if she'd had as much difficulty fending off Lee's advances as she liked to believe.

"Lettie, Delia seemed to think Lee was serious about Amanda Count. I mean, she was more than a passing fancy."

"Oh, he was serious about her," she said with a fastidious sniff. "Lee was at that dangerous age for a man when Amanda come into his life. Middle age was creepin' up on him, and Amanda was a beautiful *young* woman. And she could give him children. Delia tell you about Clare?" Then at Conan's nod, " 'Nother thing, Amanda—well, she was soft and pretty to look at, but hard as nails on the inside. She knew what she wanted, and nothin' in the world was goin' to keep her from gettin' it."

"Why did she want Lee so much?"

Lettie paused with her mouth open, and when she replied it was with pained patience. "Well, he was a big, good-lookin' man just oozin' charm. Besides, he treated her like a princess. Fancy gifts and things. Oh, she liked that."

Conan took a puff on his cigarette to mask his amusement. "Yes, I suppose any woman would like that."

Lettie's reaction was a brief, uncharacteristic hesitation, then a nervous shrug. "Well, I s'pose so."

"Was Lee at all secretive about his relationship with Amanda?"

"Secretive! He didn't seem to give a damn *who* knew. Even around the office—why, you should've seen them two, givin' each other looks, slippin' behind a closed door whenever they could. He even used to call her by his pet name for her once in a while. 'Mimi.' Silly, if you ask me."

"Mimi? Maybe he was a Puccini fan."

"A what?"

"Uh . . . nothing. It seems strange—especially in a small town—that Clare wouldn't hear about Lee's extracurricular activities sooner or later."

"She heard about it. Course, that wasn't till about a week before Lee and Amanda was plannin' to run off together. Trouble with Clare, she really didn't *want* to know. Jest kept her head in the clouds most of the time."

Conan leaned back, eyes narrowing. "But she *did* know about Amanda?"

"Sure, she did. *I* told her." Then she added defensively, "Well, I figgered she deserved to know what was goin' on. Ever'body else kept quiet about it to her, as if that was doin' her a *favor*. Mind you, I didn't say a word till about a week before. That's when Amanda come back from a trip to Boise with a set of luggage—real leather—and enough clothes and lacy underwear to open a dry goods store. She showed it to Mrs. Sparrow, her landlady. I knew good and well she didn't pay for that stuff out of her own salary, and luggage meant she was plannin' on a trip. That's when I told Clare. I figgered she had a right to know."

"What was her reaction?"

"Oh, she jest got real quiet, then she sort of laughed. Told me not to worry about Lee; he'd get tired of Amanda and come back to her. 'He'll come back,' she said. 'He always has.' Oh, there's that California woman. The photographer." Lettie was looking out the window, and Conan, following the direction of her gaze, saw Mrs. Bonnet, camera in hand, a leather case over her right shoulder, walking away from the school down Morning Star.

He asked, "Have you met Mrs. Bonnet, Lettie?"

"Nope. Hasn't been in to see the museum yet. Odd, too. Most of the newspaper and magazine people *start out* here."

"It seems a logical starting point. How long has she been in Silver?"

"Three or four days, I think. Oh-oh, here comes a bunch with kids. Y'know, I like kids, and I figger it's good for 'em seein' what we got here, but I sure wish their folks would teach 'em some manners."

Conan watched the family—with their three under-ten children—ambling toward the school from the north. "Lettie, what can you tell me about Reuben Sickle?"

"Reub?" She turned and looked at Conan curiously. "Well, not much. Don't think anybody really knows much about him. You hear about him and Clare?"

"You mean his unrequited love for her?"

"Whatever. He's a real nice fella, always has been, and

Lee used to have ever'body in town laughin' at poor ol' Reub 'cause of the way he felt about Clare. Too bad Lee didn't feel half of what Reub did for her.'' Lettie paused, brow ridged in thought. ''Y'know, I seem to remember some sort of run-in Reub had with Lee a little while before the murder. Yep, those folks are comin' in. Tell you what, you ask the Roseberrys about Reub. They know him better'n anybody else. He gets all his supplies from them.''

Conan heard voices from downstairs and rose. ''The store is my next stop anyway.''

''Here—you might as well take this.'' She handed him her muddled version of a floor plan.

''Oh, yes.'' He mustered an appreciative smile as he folded it and put it in his shirt pocket. ''Thanks, Lettie. You've been a great help.''

''Hope so. 'Bout time this thing got settled, after all these years.''

As Conan walked down Morning Star toward the bridge, he was considering Lettie's helpfulness and thinking ruefully that the investigation business had an unfortunate tendency to nurture cynicism. Whenever he encountered witnesses who seemed too eager to help, he found himself wondering about their motivation.

CHAPTER 9

When Conan walked into the General Store he had first to adjust his eyes to the dim light, then to adjust his consciousness to the out-of-time feeling of the place, which, apparently more by unconcern than intention, was so much a period piece. The uneven floor was of unvarnished planks, the advertisements on the walls vintage style and yellow with age, the limited stock included items such as lamp chimneys and washboards. The modernity of familiar brands of canned foods, soft drinks, beer, candy, and prepared meats somehow failed to update their surroundings.

He had also to adjust to finding himself confronted with a living Tweedledee and Tweedledum, one of whom happened to be female. The Roseberrys, Vernon and Margaret, were short of stature and broad of girth, with white hair, pink faces, and bright blue eyes, and so similar in appearance it was as if during their many years of constant proximity, they had molded themselves in each other's image.

They were behind the counter, side by side, when Conan entered, and both wished him a good afternoon almost in unison, then Maggie got in first with, "You must be Mr. Flagg."

He crossed to the counter. "Yes, I am. And you are none other than the Roseberrys."

They laughed, and Vern said, "Sure are. By the way, we was wonderin' . . ."

"Yes," Maggie chimed in, "about Clare. Why, she took out of here like she'd seen a ghost."

Conan said guardedly, "Well, Delia told me Clare's been under quite a strain lately."

Maggie pursed her cherubic lips. "Oh, she has, poor thing. . . ."

"What with Lee bein' found dead, y'know," Vern augmented. "Well, what can we do for you, Mr. Flagg?"

"I have a grocery list from Delia," Conan said, "and I'd like to ask you some questions."

Maggie's eyes flashed. " 'Bout the murder? Well, you just ask away. . . ."

"Right," Vern put in with a decisive nod, "we'll help any way we can. Told Delia that. We knew Tom Starbuck, and sayin' he killed Lee—that's just all wrong."

Conan nodded. "I'm working on that premise." Then before they could comment on that, he began asking his questions, and in light of their willingness to answer any and all of them, it was doubly disappointing that they knew so little about what had actually transpired on the night of September 22, 1940. Their information was entirely in agreement with what he had already learned but added nothing new.

Not until he brought up Reuben Sickle. The Roseberrys had served as Reub's source of supplies and as a bank of sorts for years; Reub seldom ventured out of the Owyhees—although Vern reported that he had bought a jeep ten years ago after his last burro died—and Vern regularly took Reub's monthly collection of gold from his placer operations to the bank in Homedale to exchange for cash. "Why, ol' Reub's got nearly fifty thousand socked away in the bank, but I don't think he has any idea how much is there. . . ."

Maggie concluded, "Or what to do with it. The state'll end up with it, probably. Don't figger he has a will, nor a soul to will it *to*."

Conan shook his head in commiseration, then, "I under-

stand Reub and Lee Langtry didn't get along well, that there
was some sort of disagreement between them not long before
the murder.''

Maggie's pink face compressed with a scornful grimace,
and Vern nodded portentously as he said, ''You bet there
was.''

''Just an awful thing,'' Maggie declared. ''That's how
Reub got that terrible scar on his face.''

''Broken bottle,'' Vern added. ''That's the sort of fella
Lee Langtry was. . . .''

''As if his fists wasn't enough! You should've seen Clare,
Mr. Flagg, after what Lee done to her that last night.''

Conan felt the conversation slipping out of his control and
asked, ''Lee and Reub had a fight, then?''

Vern nodded, leaning across the counter. ''They sure as
heck did. Over Clare, really, 'cept it was Amanda set the
thing off. Well, not direc'ly . . .''

''But it was all on her account. . . .''

''Right. Well, what happened is Reub come into town to
pick up supplies, and he usually stayed for a few beers at the
Idaho Hotel and didn't head home till after dark.''

''Then he had to chase after that critter of his,'' Maggie
reminded Vern. ''His burro. That was . . .''

''Deluxe,'' Vern supplied with a musing smile. ''Reub
called him Deluxe. Fool thing'd never stay put, even when
he was tied down. Chew right through the tether. Anyhow,
that night Reub found Deluxe over on Washington Street
chompin' on Mrs. Sparrow's marigolds.''

''And that's when the trouble commenced,'' Maggie said,
taking up the narrative. ''Reub saw Lee and Amanda on the
back stairs of the boarding house smoochin' up a storm.
Well, Reub flew mad and started callin' Lee names. . . .''

''Couldn't've called him nothin' he didn't deserve,'' Vern
assured Conan. ''I guess Lee didn't pay much attention to
him then. Amanda went on inside, and Lee headed over to
the Idaho, with Reub right after him. . . .''

''Course, Reub had a lot of beer in him. . . .''

''Or he would've done better when the fight started. That

wasn't till they was both in the bar at the hotel. Even then, the way I heard it, Reub got a few good licks in."

Maggie sighed gustily. "That prob'ly just got Lee all the madder. He took after Reub with a broken bottle. . . ."

"Slashed him right across the face. Well, you seen him, didn't you, Mr. Flagg? Just missed blindin' him."

"Awful thing," Maggie insisted. "Why, Lee would've killed poor Reub if some of the fellas in the bar hadn't stopped him. Reub took off for his cabin, and how he lived through the next few days, I'll never know. Weren't a doctor around. . . ."

"Don't figger he'd've gone to one anyhow. . . ."

"And he had to take care of that gash himself. Wouldn't let nobody near him. Even took a shot at Vern one day when he tried to go up to the cabin."

Vern shrugged at that. "He was just shootin' into the air. Didn't mean no real harm."

"Vern left medicine and bandages and food for him on the road below his place ever' few days afterward."

Conan asked, "How long did he stay in hiding?"

Vern looked at Maggie for confirmation as he replied, "Well, it was about three months altogether before he finally come into town."

"In the *day*time," Maggie amended. "But folks said they saw him around town at night—remember, Vern?—right after the fight, oh, for about a month. Well, up till the robbery when Lee and Amanda disappeared. We kept hearin' stories about how people seen him prowlin' around after dark, him with his face all bandaged up, and his rifle—always carried that rifle, even before that. Still does. Anyway, some folks thought he was a ghost. . . ."

"Leastways," Vern put in with a laugh, "if they'd had a bit to drink when they saw him."

Conan smiled at that. "Did you see him during that period?"

"No, Maggie and me was always early-to-bed and early-to-rise people. Nobody ever claimed to see Reub 'cept at night. Most folks figgered he was lookin' for Lee."

Conan ventured, "Maybe he found him, finally."

At that, both the Roseberrys were aghast. Maggie asked, "You don't think *Reub* killed Lee, do you? Oh, Mr. Flagg, I can't believe—I mean Reub . . ."

Vern declared, "Reub wouldn't've *killed* him. He'd darn sure tried to beat the blazes out of him, but that's all."

Conan nodded agreement because he saw that Vern and Maggie found themselves confronted with a new idea, one they didn't like, and he hoped to avoid shutting off one of his few willing sources of information. "Reub strikes me as a man more inclined to use his fists than a knife. When did you say this fight took place?"

Vern was apparently reassured. "Well, near as I can recollect, it was almost exactly a month before the robbery."

Maggie nodded then, "Yes, that's right. Oh, that poor man, what he must've suffered all by himself up in that cabin. Why, he should've been in a hospital with a gash like that. Must've hurt somethin' awful."

Both physically and emotionally, Conan added to himself, and Reub would have no trouble carrying Lee's body from the office to the mine and no trouble finding the adit. He probably knew the location of every shaft and adit in the Owyhees.

It was nearly six o'clock when Conan left the store with Delia's groceries. The clouds were an unbroken ceiling pressing upon the backs of the mountains and hurrying the twilight; the wind had died, and he seemed to be the only thing moving in the landscape. When he reached the Starbuck house, he took the groceries to the kitchen, where he found Delia stoking up the wood stove.

He asked, "Where's Clare?"

Delia thrust another stick of wood into the firebox, then closed the door with a sharp clang. "Oh, she took the food to her grove. Left about fifteen minutes ago."

"Alone?"

"She didn't want me tagging along this time." Delia turned to the sack Conan had put on the table. "Thanks for bringing these. You have a good talk with the Roseberrys?"

"Yes, and with Lettie." The coffee pot was still warming

at the back of the stove; he filled a mug and sat down at the table with it, while Delia took the sack to the counter and began emptying it. "Delia, Lettie told me Dex Adler was in serious financial trouble before the robbery, but he apparently had an extremely opportune windfall that got him out of trouble soon afterward."

She unwrapped the chicken and examined it closely. "I told you Lettie knew a lot about other people's business."

Conan waited for her to answer his implicit question, but she seemed very busy putting groceries in the refrigerator. He made the question explicit. "*Did* Dex have an opportune windfall, Delia? And, please, don't tell me to ask him about it."

She smiled faintly as she closed the refrigerator. "Conan, I know what you're wondering about. You think maybe Dex's windfall came out of the Lang-Star safe, and if it did, then maybe Dex is the one who killed Lee—right?"

"Well, it's a possibility."

"No, it's not. Not even a possibility. So, that's one thing you don't have to worry about." And with that assurance, she picked up the empty sack and began folding it.

Conan sipped at his coffee. "Delia, I need more than that to eliminate the possibility."

She put the sack in a drawer, the lines around her mouth tight. "I can't give you more, Conan. Except, like I told you, only Tom and Lee knew the combination to the safe."

"But Dex was the bookkeeper; he handled the company funds."

"He didn't handle them in or out of that safe."

Conan studied her a moment, then nodded, recognizing a stone wall when he ran up against it. He turned to another subject. Or suspect? No, not yet. "How did Lettie get along with Lee?"

Delia crossed her arms as she leaned back against the counter. "Well, I never heard her say anything *good* about him. The best she ever had to say was—how did she put it?— 'Too damn good-lookin' and sweet-talkin' by a long shot.' "

Conan smiled, hearing those words in Lettie's sour, disapproving tones. "Did he ever try sweet-talking her?"

Delia raised both eyebrows. "I doubt that very much." Then after a moment, she added, "And I doubt Lettie appreciated being ignored."

"Perhaps she protests too much about Lee."

"She did then. But that's just my opinion. I don't know how she really felt about him. All I know is she always seemed to keep close track of everything he did. Well, I guess I'd better get started on supper."

Conan came to his feet. "Unless you'll accept my assistance at that, I'll take a shower."

"No, I won't accept any of your assistance, so go on. Holler if you need anything."

Conan found himself rushing through his shower, and he couldn't explain the brooding anxiety that seemed to lurk in the shadows at the back of his mind. The prestorm heat, perhaps; the low barometric pressure. It wasn't until he returned to the kitchen half an hour later that he realized what in particular was bothering him, not until he asked Delia, "Isn't Clare back yet?"

Delia was tending a big iron skillet sputtering with frying chicken. She glanced up at the clock, frowning. "No, she's not, but she stays out till dark sometimes."

"It's nearly dark now with the clouds coming in."

Delia nodded. "I think you'd better go look for her. That's what you were leading up to, wasn't it?"

Conan was already on his way out. "Yes."

He was no more than fifty yards from the house when he heard the shots. It was almost an exact repetition of the previous evening, except for the electric quality of the air, the saffron light reflected from the pending clouds. He set off at a run across the gullied slopes, and by the time he reached the road up Slaughterhouse Gulch, he was panting in the rarefied air.

He found Clare lying huddled on the ground near the road, sobbing pitifully, her face and clothing smeared with dirt, her small hands clutching at the gravel.

"Clare!" He knelt beside her; she didn't seem to be hurt. "Clare, what happened?"

"Kill me . . . tried to . . . Delia, oh, help . . ."

That was as close as he was to get to an explanation; she broke into renewed sobbing, the only coherent word her sister's name. Conan picked her up and carried her to the house, while she clung to him, face buried against his shoulder, and he doubted she had the faintest awareness of who he was.

The storm broke at 1 A.M. with explosions of lightning and thunder cracking against the mountain faces; drenching rains rattled on the metal roof. Conan heard Clare, waking, cry out in fear. A few minutes later, he saw a light under the hall door: Delia crossing to Clare's room.

He rose and lit a cigarette, then opened the balcony door. The rain-laden wind was clean and cold, and he could feel the vibrations of thunder under his bare feet. He looked out at the town intermittently washed in blue-white light, and thought of Clare, of the terrors inflicted on her, the imagined ones worse than the real. And he thought of age, thought of choices.

Would anyone, given a choice, not choose to grow old with the indomitable grace of Cordelia Becket Starbuck? Who would choose to live in the warped, unfocused world that was Clare Langtry's lot?

But who was ever given such a choice?

CHAPTER 10

The storm spent itself during the night, and by morning the sky was clear, the blossoming crab apples magnificent against its flawless blue, the ground beneath them snowed with white petals. Conan left the house armed with a mental map supplied by Delia that would, with a little luck, guide him to the mine adit where Lee Langtry's body had been discovered. He paused at the foot of the porch steps to savor the scents of wet earth and sage, and it seemed he had suddenly acquired the sight of a hawk, so clear was the mountain air.

"Halloooo!"

He frowned, refocusing his new sight at a point just beyond the crab apples. That friendly greeting came from Betty Potter, ensconced in her director's chair among her artistic paraphernalia. She was waving a brush and smiling, and, since it seemed unavoidable, he walked over to her. "Good morning, Mrs. Potter." The showy, diamonded wedding ring hinted that she would consider "Ms." an insult.

"Isn't it a *glorious* morning? You're Conan Flagg, aren't you? Jake told me." Then with a titter, "Well, I *had* to find out who that handsome man staying at the Starbuck house was. A private investigator—oh, that's so exciting!"

"Not really," Conan replied, looking down at the work in progress. Mrs. Potter had switched to watercolor, which was unfortunate. That underestimated and difficult medium fared badly at her hands. He quickly looked away, fearing an inquiry for an opinion.

It wasn't long in coming. "Well, what do you think, Mr. Flagg? I felt those trees really *demanded* a watercolor treatment, you know. They're so incredibly subtle. I mean, you look at them and think *white*, but there are a thousand colors in that white."

And she seemed determined to work every one of them into a pallid mud. Conan mustered a smile. "I admire your daring, Mrs. Potter. Watercolor isn't easy under the best of circumstances."

"Oh, it's a challenge, but I always say—" She stopped, distracted by a click and whir. On the road behind them, Mrs. Bonnet stood with the blank eye of her camera lens fixed on them.

Another click and whir, then she walked toward them, negotiating the hummocky road nicely in her high wedge shoes. She was wearing dark glasses, as usual, a Panama straw hat, and denim slacks and jacket remotely inspired by Levi Strauss, but removed from his original by several hundred dollars. Her leather camera bag was slung over one shoulder, and the camera, Conan noted, was an impressive Nikon F2A 35 mm.

"What a great shot!" she commented as she approached. "Artist and kibitzer, those beautiful trees, and that terrific old house."

Betty Potter tittered again. "Be *sure* and let me know when your article comes out. Won't my friends be *jealous*!"

"Don't ever count your pictures until the editor has passed judgment, Betty." Then she looked up at Conan and offered a hand. "I'm Mimi Bonnet. I'm here doing an article for *Sunset Magazine*."

Conan shook hands with her. "Conan Flagg. Yes, I've heard about you." And what he had heard was that she was doing a picture page for the Los Angeles *Times*. "Mimi, did you say? That's an unusual name."

Her mouth smiled, but her shaded eyes were an enigma. "I seem to be stuck with it. Well, I'd better be on my way. Can't waste this fantastic light." She walked on up the road by the house, stopping intermittently to snap more pictures. She seemed oddly casual about it; at least, she spent very little time framing her shots.

Mrs. Potter speculated, "Maybe she'd let me have some of the pictures she doesn't use for her article. They'd be just marvelous for painting."

Conan tried not to groan. "I'm sure she'd be willing to forward the cause of art. Well, I'd better be on my way, too. Good luck, Mrs. Potter."

"Off to do some *investigating*, Mr. Flagg?"

"Something like that."

He headed north and a little east, passing within a short distance of Adler's house. Adler, pointedly oblivious to Conan's proximity, was hammering at a shutter on one of the front windows. Conan crossed Slaughterhouse Gulch above Clare's grove. Under his feet flecks of mica glittered in the sunlight. Clare's stars. He found a few rusted, hand-forged square nails along the way, but left them where they lay. The little church gleamed white on the slope below him, and he paused to look down on it. There was a sturdy optimism about it, as there was about the entire town from this point. It survived with no discernible purpose to justify its existence, except perhaps the satisfaction of curiosity.

He looked up at the mountain of tailings that marked the site of the Lang-Star mill; it towered above him now, a still, white avalanche. Perhaps the satisfaction of curiosity was ample purpose. And did existence—or life—require justification, when the alternative was nonexistence or death?

He smiled to—and at—himself, and turned his thoughts to the mundane problem of finding the path that Delia had assured him lay east of the tailings. He encountered a collapsed mine adit, but it wasn't *the* mine. Juniper and mountain mahogany grew thicker as the slope behind the tailings steepened, and he began to wonder if he'd have to go back and recruit Delia as a pathfinder. But at length he found the path. At least, *a* path, winding up the base of War Eagle toward a

massive outcropping of granite. He stopped in the shade of
a juniper and looked back. The mill site was below him now,
and he considered the difficulty of finding this path at night,
of traversing it while laden with the body of a large man. It
made less and less sense, but Lee's body *had* been carried
over this route somehow.

He caught a movement out of the corner of his eye; something in the trees near the tailings. Yet when he examined the
area he saw nothing, nor did he hear anything except a warm
wind sighing in the juniper above him. He shrugged and
continued up the path.

Half an hour later, he reached a grove of aspen and took
advantage of their shade to catch his breath. The leaves of
the trees shimmered around him, their intense green presag-
ing the incandescent gold of autumn. A whistling cry made
him look up, and he saw an eagle plying the wind above him
in slow, sinuous spirals. Again he was reminded of Clare,
but he found it difficult to think of Lee Langtry in terms of
a golden eagle. The Lee Langtry Conan had come to know
had nothing in common with the eagle except its predatory
nature, and the eagle had no choice in that.

A short time later—after laboriously gaining another two-
hundred feet in elevation—Conan reached the object of his
search. He was alerted by a faded sign nailed to the trunk of
a juniper. It proclaimed the area posted by the Owyhee
County Sheriff.

He stayed on the path, and beyond the next curve, it deliv-
ered him, at last, to the adit. A horizontal passage had been
blasted into the mountainside; for thirty feet it was simply
an open chute, the walls increasing in height until the channel became a tunnel disappearing into the mountain. He made
his way up the channel, the granite walls rising on both sides
of him, into the dark mouth of the tunnel. A cool breeze
blew out of it, and within the stone was patched with moss.
There were even, in this arid climate, clumps of tiny ferns
growing in the rocky interstices.

He took off his sunglasses and stood facing the dark interior while his eyes adjusted, and then he could see that the
tunnel ended only twenty feet away. Rather, access to its

further reaches was blocked. He walked slowly toward the barrier of boards where a white-on-red sign warned him to keep out. He had no intention of defying that silent order, but he went all the way to the barrier. One of the boards had been pried loose, probably by sightseers.

Not that there was a great deal to see; the only light came from the break in the boards, and the tunnel was soon swallowed up in absolute blackness. The body had lain on the rocky floor just beyond the barrier—he knew that from the police photographs—but there was nothing left his eye could discern to substantiate that fact. Conan felt the chill air on his face and thought of the miners who had toiled and died within those lightless passages and wondered if anything could make that life worth the price.

But he had a tendency to claustrophobia, and obviously many people had considered the rewards worth the risks. He turned and made his way back toward the light, which seemed blindingly bright now. Lee's car was the problem, he was thinking. Now that he'd seen the burial place and fully understood the difficulty of finding it, especially at night, of carrying the body here, plus taking down and restoring the barrier that had blocked the tunnel then as now, it didn't seem possible that one person could accomplish that *and* get back to the office in time to drive away in Lee's car in the hour and a half between eight-thirty, when Lee left his house for the office, and ten, when Adler went there—according to his sworn testimony—and found the car gone.

Conan frowned at that. Sworn testimony was not what he considered iron-clad evidence.

As he left the tunnel behind, he squinted against the light and reached in his shirt pocket for his sunglasses. The granite walls still enclosed him on both sides, and he heard a sound—two sounds—above him and to his right: a gravelly scraping, then something like an animal grunt.

But he didn't have time to explore the sounds or their source more closely. A swiftly moving shadow was all he saw, and something crashed against the back of his head.

Mercifully, he didn't feel a thing when he sprawled face down on the rocky ground.

CHAPTER 11

He had actually seen stars—at least, flashes of light—just like in the cartoons.

Conan lay with his cheek pressed against granite considering that phenomenon. Finally, he stirred and discovered he could lift his head, despite the painful protests of his neck muscles and a thudding headache. After he had at length maneuvered into a sitting position, it occurred to him to wonder what had hit him, and if he should be doing something to avoid getting hit again. At the moment, the only practical approach to the latter concern was absolute fatalism.

He closed his eyes while he tried to make sense of where he was and what had happened, then gingerly pressed his hand to the back of his head. He encountered a burgeoning lump, but nothing more; the skin hadn't even been broken.

The sun shone hot and bright on him, and he looked for his dark glasses, locating them finally a short distance away. He achieved an upright stance by using the granite wall as a support, then crossed the few feet to his glasses. Afterward, he decided that leaning down to pick them up was not a wise course.

Still, he seemed to be making some progress. His eyes

were staying in focus, and the pulsating ache occupying his head and lancing down his neck subsided to bearable intensity as he made his way out of the rock-rimmed channel. He could even remember going into the tunnel and looking through the broken boards, which suggested that he'd been unconscious a very short time. He couldn't remember leaving the tunnel, however, nor anything during the vital seconds before he was hit. He was sure he had been struck with malice aforethought simply because the only other explanation for the new contour of his skull was a fall. That seemed unlikely.

He searched for evidence of a human presence above the channel on both sides, but found nothing—not until he left the adit and started down the path.

The old adage that there were no straight lines in nature was a fallacy; straight lines abound in the natural world on any scale. Still, there were few in this particular landscape, and the board lying beneath a sagebrush about ten yards from the adit stood out as a startling anomaly. He walked over to it and smiled grimly.

It was a three-foot length of two-by-four, gray with age, and there was nothing unusual about it in itself. What was unusual was that one end was wrapped with a burlap sack. It hadn't been lying here long: there was very little dust in the burlap or on the string binding it.

Now he knew what had hit him, and he knew why it hadn't broken the skin. But why had his assailant been so considerate as to pad this weapon to soften the blow?

Undoubtedly the blow was primarily for effect, like the rattlesnake in his car. The effect was quite tangible and every pulsebeat brought it home to him, but it would have been far more impressive if the assailant hadn't left his padded weapon behind. That, Conan was sure, had not been intentional. He started down the path with the board in hand, anticipating the long walk back to the Starbuck house with no enthusiasm, and finding the idea of being the object of such inept intimidation disquieting. The next attempt to scare him off this case might be fatal purely by accident.

Then he came to a sudden halt, staring down at the path.

In the shade of a granite boulder, a shallow depression had caught enough of last night's rain to turn into mud, and some-one had made the error of stepping in it.

He couldn't have asked for a better medium for preservation; the mud was exactly the right consistency. Both the right and left feet were there; large feet shod in boots most likely, with a deep tread as specific as any tire tread. He found the left foot especially informative: the tread was worn almost smooth on the outside edge of the sole.

When Conan reached Slaughterhouse Gulch and crossed the treeless slope toward the Starbuck house, his head was still pounding unremittingly, but as he neared Dex Adler's house, he braced himself and put as much jauntiness in his stride as he could muster. Adler was still assiduously playing carpenter, this time on his porch step. Conan shifted the two-by-four to his left hand so Adler would be sure to see it.

"Good morning, Mr. Adler."

Adler lowered his hammer and squinted at him suspiciously, and apparently curiosity got the better of animosity. His tone was almost friendly. "Morning. Uh . . . out for a walk?"

Conan smiled but didn't break pace. "I went up to the mine adit where Lee's body was found."

"The adit? What—what's that you've got there?"

Conan hefted the board. "Oh, just a souvenir."

Adler might have had more to say, but Conan was past him now, and he knew from the silence behind him that Adler was watching him every step of the way. Conan maintained his jauntiness until he rounded the corner of the Starbuck house, but when he reached the porch he had to pause before attempting the steps to the front door.

He met Delia in the hall. She was on her way downstairs from the bedrooms, and she stopped, staring at him. "Conan, are you all right? You're white as a sheet."

He went straight to the parlor and sank into the first chair he encountered. "Delia, I need some aspirin, a glass of water, and an ice pack, if possible."

A remarkable woman, he thought gratefully; no questions,

no fuss or delay. In five minutes, she had furnished the required items. She remained calmly silent while he swallowed two aspirins, considered the matter and downed two more, then leaned back, holding the ice pack against his throbbing head.

Only then did she ask, "What happened?"

"I must've run into a door."

"That's a queer looking door." She picked up the two-by-four, which he had dropped at his feet.

He laughed. "Yes, it is. Very queer. Where's Clare?"

"Out in the garden. Who hit you, Conan?"

"I didn't see who it was." He shifted the ice pack. "That feels better. Delia, is Dex still outside his house?"

Her eyes widened, then narrowed. "I'll look." She went to the north window, then after a moment, "He's still there. Conan, you don't think *Dex* hit you. He couldn't have. He's been out there hammering away for more than an hour. I heard him."

"No, I don't think he hit me."

"Then, who did?"

"I don't know." That wasn't quite true, but he didn't want to discuss it now. Then he looked up at her, aware of her uneasy silence. "Delia, it isn't serious. Don't worry about it."

"Don't worry!" She gave a little snort of disgust. "This sort of thing wasn't part of my arrangement with you. I didn't ask you to come here to . . . to run into doors."

Conan pulled himself to his feet and crossed to the window. "An occupational hazard, Delia, but thanks for offering me a graceful exit. I don't need it, however. Do you?"

She pursed her lips. "No. Not yet, anyway. Well, it's almost time for lunch. You feel like eating something?"

Conan didn't answer immediately. He was watching Dex Adler; he had gone inside his house, but left his front door open. "No, Delia, I'm not hungry."

"Maybe a stiff shot of whiskey, then."

"That's probably not a good idea." Adler reappeared at his door and stood looking about indecisively.

"Conan, maybe the best idea would be to have a doctor look at you. There's one in Homedale."

"No, that's not necessary." Adler seemed to square his shoulders, then left his house and walked south at a brisk pace. Conan turned from the window and gave Delia a reassuring smile. "I doubt I've sustained any serious damage. By the way, didn't you say Reub Sickle lives up Jordan Creek?"

She replied warily, "Yes, he has a cabin up there not far from the creek."

Finding Reub's cabin was a great deal easier than finding the mine adit, and Conan took it on foot and at a leisurely pace. That seemed the only sensible course out of consideration for his swelling head.

Just walk south on the Jordan Creek road, Delia had instructed him, and about half a mile out of town you'll come to a road that goes down to a ford over the creek. About a quarter of a mile past the ford, the road forks, and you take the left-hand road. It goes up a little valley, and that's where you'll find Reub's place.

It was still a glorious day, and Conan ambled down Jordan Creek road with the stream murmuring behind the willows on his left. On his right the slopes of Potosi Peak were splashed with lupine, scarlet gilia, orange globe mallow, and the multitudinous little suns of balsam. He followed Delia's directions as far as the second junction of roads—and "road" was a marginally accurate term for furrowed trails—but beyond that point he struck out on his own. He climbed the side of the valley, keeping the road that led to Reub's cabin in sight below him. He soon found himself in groves of aspen, their trunks ghost-white against the rich, blued green of subalpine fir. The sound of the wind in the firs wakened something akin to homesickness in him, it was so much like the sighing of surf outside his window at home.

At length, he saw a small cabin below, board-and-batten walls weathered into a tapestry of gold and umber. Reub had chosen a beautiful setting for his little home, facing west with War Eagle at its back, surrounded by a meadow bright with wild flowers. Behind the cabin was a slope-roofed outhouse and a sagging shed. A flat roof shaded the porch that spanned the entire front of the cabin, and a battered jeep was parked before it, as if hitched to the corner post.

Conan moved cautiously downslope to the edge of the meadow, but when he heard a warning bark and saw a black dog of mixed ancestry—predominantly Lab, probably—and unmistakable territorial instinct rise from the shade of the jeep, Conan sank down behind a young fir, grateful that the wind was in his favor. The dog sniffed the air in every direction, put in another bark as the last word, then lay down in front of the door to guard it.

The door opened a few minutes later, and even at a distance of at least two hundred feet, Conan clearly heard Reub Sickle's gruff, "Hey, Sheba, move over, you ol' mutt."

Sheba did, wagging her tail and putting her head up for an affectionate rub when Reub came out on the porch. "I'm goin' over town for supplies. You want a ride down?"

But that wasn't for Sheba; Reub was looking back at the man who emerged from the cabin behind him.

"All right, Reub," Dex Adler said, frowning absently at the dog, then at the jeep as he followed Reub. He was still frowning when Reub turned the jeep and lurched away down the road. Sheba was in the back, grinning happily, ears flying.

CHAPTER 12

Before he made himself guilty of breaking and entering—
and in this case it would only be entering; there was no lock
on Reub's door—Conan scouted around the cabin for bare
patches of earth still damp enough to hold footprints. Near
the front porch he found several of Reub's prints—exact du-
plicates of the ones near the mine adit, with the tell-tale
smoothness at the outside of the left sole produced by Reub's
malformed ankle. Conan also found the slightly smaller
tracks made by Dex Adler's Wallaboes.

At the back of the cabin he found another set of tracks that
were far more intriguing: they were small, with a rippled
pattern, and their shape was unusual; rather like a bowling
pin in vertical cross-section. A woman's high-heeled, wedge-
soled shoe. No doubt Reub's cabin was very photogenic, but
it seemed a little outside the purview of an article on Silver
City.

When Conan went inside the cabin, he left the door open.
There was only the one room, its walls, floor, and ceiling all
of rough pine, and it was remarkably tidy. A broom and
dustpan stood in one corner, and the windows were curtained
in faded flour-sacking. The narrow bed, with its thin, con-

cave mattress, was neatly made up under a gray wool blanket. On the right-hand wall was a wood-burning cookstove, which apparently served as Reub's heat source as well, and in the front corner near the stove, a plank counter supported a washbasin and water pail. The shelves beneath the counter were filled with sacks of flour, beans, sugar, and cornmeal, boxes of raisins, dried milk, a variety of canned goods, a sourdough crock, and such necessities as coffee and tobacco. There was also, Conan noted, a first-aid and snake-bite kit. A calendar, courtesy of the Wagon Wheel in Murphy, was nailed to the wall by the stove. It was two years out of date.

On the left-hand wall, in open shelves and hung on nails, was an assortment of tools: shovels, pickax, rock picks, sledge hammer, maul, long-handled ax, gold pans, mortar and pestle, mineral-stained crucibles. Near the door hung a pair of snowshoes and a sheepskin jacket, and occupying the center of the cabin was a wooden table flanked by two chairs. There were no books, no pictures, no means of communication with the outside world, and little that even hinted at its existence. Yet here was a man's entire life neatly stored in one small room, and Conan didn't doubt that Reuben Sickle was satisfied with his life. A fortunate man, perhaps.

Conan searched the cabin thoroughly, but without leaving a trace. He'd been trained for that, but no amount of training could make him feel comfortable about invading another person's privacy. He could only assure himself that in some cases, at least, the ends justify the means. In this case, his aching head provided further justification.

But Reub apparently had nothing to hide, or he had hidden it elsewhere. Conan had nearly given up when he realized that one of the floorboards behind the stove had been sawed, then laid back in place. He used a table knife to pry it up and within the earthen cavity beneath found a small, wooden box with a metal hasp and a padlock securing the lid.

But he wasn't the first to discover this box. The hasp had been pried loose, making the padlock a useless appendage.

He took the box to the table to open it and found only two objects within it. The first was a cameo brooch with a female head in profile set in a gold filigree mounting.

The second was a nickel-plated .38 revolver.

Conan examined the gun closely. It was fully loaded, but he doubted it had been fired recently; there were spots of corrosion not only within the barrel but even on the cartridge casings. Some identifying marks had been scratched on the butt. He frowned over them and finally deciphered the letters LL. Leland Langtry, perhaps?

Conan reexamined the brooch, but there was nothing to indicate its owner's identity. Still frowning, he checked the interior of the box, noting a few tiny scraps of brittle, yellowed paper. One seemed to be the corner of a sheet.

He heard the distant rumble of a motor and a bucking rattling. Reub's jeep. The usual course would be to replace the box and make a quick exit, but he chose to stay.

Reub Sickle had some explaining to do.

When Reub opened the door, Conan was standing behind the table with the .38 leveled at him. The box was still open on the table.

Sheba was the first to recover from the initial surprise. She danced about in a fury of barking, and Reub, glaring from Conan to the gun, reached down with his left hand to restrain her. His right hand was occupied with his rifle. "Quiet, Sheba. Jest hold on, now. . . ."

Sheba subsided with a warning growl, and Reub's eyes shifted to the box. The scar flawing his face seemed to turn whiter as his face reddened. "What the hell're you doin'' with—you got no right—"

"No, but I have this gun," Conan noted. "Reub, I'm not out for blood, but I could damn sure put you in a hospital."

Reub seemed to consider that, eyeing Conan speculatively. "That thing's li'ble to blow up in your face if you pull the trigger. Hasn't been fired in over forty years."

"You want to take that chance, Reub?" Apparently he didn't; his wide shoulders sagged, and when Conan ordered, "Put your rifle here on the table, then back off," Reub quieted the restive Sheba again, then approached the table and laid the rifle on it. But outrage overwhelmed discretion when he looked into the box.

He cried, "Where's the—you *stole* it! You gawdamned—"

Conan pulled the rifle out of Reub's reach and raised the .38 a few inches as a reminder. "You mean the letter?"

"You—you know damn well . . ." Then he stopped, his big hands curling at his sides. "I got nothin' to say to you. Jest get outa my place! You got what you wanted!"

"No, I didn't, Reub, and all I want is some answers. *I* didn't open this box. This is exactly the way I found it, and the only thing I've removed from it is this gun."

Sheba growled and showed her teeth, and Reub stood in granitic silence, unimpressed and unconvinced. Conan sighed wearily, but gave it another try. "Reub, why do you think I'm still here? I heard you coming in plenty of time to get out of here—with the whole damned box. And I have ample reason to press assault charges against you, and one hell of a headache that makes that sound like a good idea." That shook Reub, but not enough to induce him to take a more cooperative attitude. Conan demanded, "What's missing from this box?"

Still, stoic silence; Reub's fisted hands didn't relax.

Conan nodded at the .38. "This is Lee Langtry's gun, isn't it? Where did you find it? And when? Damn it, Reub, you're only making things worse."

There was a fleeting—and revealing—movement in the tense muscles around Reub's mouth at Lee's name, and he finally spoke, but not to answer Conan's questions.

"Mister, you get outa here, or by Gawd, I'll sic Sheba on you—gun or no!" The dog seconded that with another growl.

Conan irritably slammed the box shut and reached for the rifle. "Give me the keys to the jeep."

Reub's blue eyes widened in candid bewilderment. "The keys are in the—" Then he caught himself. "What d'you want the keys for?"

"Never mind. Get over there by the bed. Move!" His peremptory tone worked. Reub shuffled warily toward the bed, while Conan moved around the table in the opposite direction. "Keep that dog with you. That's right. Lie down on the floor. Do it, Reub!" He waited while Reub reluctantly did as he was ordered, with Sheba, nonplussed, trying to lick at his face. Conan put down an urge to laugh, concentrating on keeping his tone terse and uncompromising. "Now, slide under the bed."

Reub spluttered, "Damn you, Flagg, what the hell—Sheba, get away—"

"*Under* the bed, Reub!" Then, when that was finally accomplished, Conan thrust the .38 into his belt and grabbed one of the chairs. As he went out the door he said, "I'll leave the jeep and your rifle at the hotel, Reub."

An explosion of profanity and barking answered that. Conan hurriedly shut the door, left the chair on its side in front of it, then sprinted for the jeep. The keys were in the ignition, and to his relief the motor responded immediately. He had lurched a good hundred yards down the road when he looked back and saw Reub burst out of his door and fall headlong over the chair. A moment later he was up again, shouting and waving his arms, while Sheba hurtled after the jeep in noisy pursuit, but Conan was out of sight around the first curve in the road.

CHAPTER 13

Conan parked the jeep at the south end of the Idaho Hotel's long porch near Mrs. Bonnet's white Cadillac, laid the rifle out of sight on the floorboards, then pulled his shirt down over the .38 in his belt, hoping to at least disguise the obvious bulge.

John Kulik and his friend Bill Cobb were lounging on one of the old church pews near the hotel door. They smiled, but John's eyes went immediately to the jeep. He observed casually, "That's Reub Sickle's jeep."

Conan nodded. "He'll be down to pick it up soon. Is your father inside?"

"Yes, in the dining room, or he may be back in the kitchen. Just holler for him."

"Thanks." Conan started for the door, but paused there. "By the way, have you seen Mrs. Bonnet lately?"

John frowned questioningly, and it was Bill who asked bluntly, "Why?"

"I just wanted to talk to her. She promised me a print of one of her pictures of the Starbuck house."

That seemed to assuage their curiosity. John replied unconcernedly, "She left a little while ago. Said she was going over to the Potosi mill site on Long Gulch."

"I'll catch her later." Conan went into the hotel, his entrance heralded by the tinkling of the bells mounted on the door. A young couple—tourists, apparently—looked up from their perusal of a display case, smiled, then returned to their study. Otherwise, the lobby, which now did multiple duty as a museum and antique shop, was unoccupied. Conan crossed to the double doors opening into the dining room.

That Jake Kulik had been working under the most adverse of circumstances was obvious. The marbled green wallpaper was faded and peeling, the ceiling and wood floor sagging, and there was a hint of mustiness in the cool air that reminded Conan of the draft expelled from the mine tunnel. Yet Kulik had, as Delia put it, done wonders. Eight large, vintage tables, polished surfaces gleaming, stood ready to serve diners, as they had a century ago, while lamps with delicately painted shades stood ready to light their evenings. The tall, narrow windows on the far wall looked east over Jordan Creek, and their light enhanced the display of glass bottles crowding the shelves inserted between the frames. On the right wall, occupying half the length of the room, was a mahogany bar complete with brass railing, and behind it a magnificent mirrored back bar, its numerous niches and shelves filled with more bottles. The bottles were not themselves filled, and most bore price marks. The bar no longer served as a dispensary for liquor, but for nostalgia.

Conan wandered around the room, eyes ranging over china cabinets and sideboards, an oak ice box, an upright piano with copper reliefs representing—probably—Beethoven and Mozart, a coin-operated match-vending machine, and a wheel of fortune gambling machine, also coin-operated. But the *pièce de résistance* was an oil painting on the wall between the door and the bar: the inevitable barroom nude. An odalisque, no less, remotely reminiscent of Ingres, depicting a reclining nude with rather unlikely anatomy. Two equally unlikely cherubs impended above her.

"Mr. Flagg? Didn't hear you come in." Jake Kulik pushed through the swinging doors on the north wall, boots thumping as he crossed to Conan, offering a hand and a broad smile. "Well, now, what can I do for you? Want a menu? Don't have much on it 'cept soup and sandwiches, but they're not bad, if I do say so."

Conan smiled. "I don't doubt it, but I'm afraid I'll have to explore your cuisine some other time, Jake."

"Hey, I know what's the matter with you. You figger I can't come up to Delia's cookin'. Well, you're right about that. Cup of coffee, maybe?"

"Thanks, but I'll have to put that off, too." He paused, turning sober and lowering his voice slightly. "Jake, you know Delia hired me to investigate Lee Langtry's murder, don't you?"

Kulik crossed well-muscled arms while he gave Conan his intent attention. "Yep, I know. You havin' any luck?"

Conan was aware of the headache that still pounded dully. "Of a sort. I'm going to ask some questions and ask a favor of you that may seem out of line, but I can only give you my word they're important."

At that Kulik frowned, one hand going to his beard. "Well, y'know, I'll do anything I can to help Delia out, but . . . well, what is it you want to ask?"

"What can you tell me about Mimi Bonnet?"

Kulik stared at him, then started to laugh, but seeing Conan's steadfast soberness, simply shrugged. "Mrs. Bonnet? What's she got to do with Lee Langtry?"

"Possibly nothing. I just think there's more to her than meets the eye. When did she arrive in Silver?"

"Oh . . . I guess it was last Tuesday. This is Saturday, isn't it? Right. It was five days ago. I know because she told me this mornin' she was leavin' day after tomorrow, and she wanted to pay up her bill for seven days."

Conan frowned, distracted by the bells on the front door, but it was only the young couple making their exit. "She's leaving Monday morning? Did she pay by check?"

"No. Cash. Look, Conan, all I know about her is she's from Los Angeles and she's a photographer." Then with a wry grin he added, "And she made a hundred-dollar contribution to the Silver preservation fund."

"In cash again? Jake, are your guest rooms equipped with locks?"

Kulik needed a moment to digest the implications in that, and they didn't go down well. His dark brows met in a frown. "Course they have locks. Why?"

"I want to find out more about Mrs. Bonnet, and before you call Sheriff Newbolt, I'll tell you again, I think it may be important."

"Damn it, I can't let people just walk into my guests' rooms! What d'you—I mean, I . . . damn it, Conan—"

"All right, you can't *knowingly* let people just walk in, but you're a busy man, and no one expects you to waste your time sitting in the lobby watching who comes and goes. Jake, I'm working for Delia."

It took some further convincing, but at length an agreement was reached: Kulik would simply return to work in the kitchen, and if Conan happened to find the extra keys to the rooms, which were kept behind the counter in the lobby, Kulik would be innocent of complicity. And if Conan was caught, he was entirely on his own.

The lobby was still empty when Conan purloined the key to No. 1. He learned Mimi Bonnet's room number from the register, as well as the fact that only four rooms were restored fully enough to be rented. Betty Potter was in No. 3. He frowned at that, but considered it highly unlikely that Mrs. Potter would be in her room now or in the near future. On this glorious day she was undoubtedly still at large committing painting on the landmarks of Silver City. He crossed to the front door and looked out through the lace curtains. John and Bill were still on the porch, the young couple were taking snapshots of the hotel, but no one else was in sight. He went to the door on the north wall, leaving it open when he passed into the hall behind it and climbed the stairs to the second floor.

The upper reaches of the hotel were a maze of halls and rooms, but the rental rooms were down a corridor striking north at the head of the stairs. The first on his left was No. 1, which put it at the front of the building. He unlocked the door and left it open, too; he had to be able to hear the warning of the bells on the front door downstairs.

It was a small room, and although the walnut bedstead and matching dresser would command a high price at an antique shop, the room was in all likelihood far from the standards someone of Mrs. Bonnet's apparent affluence was accustomed to in lodgings. Still, in this setting the water-spotted, flowered wallpaper, the unfinished wood floor, and the limp curtains could charitably be called charming, and at any rate, Mrs. Bonnet didn't have much choice in Silver, unless she wanted to pitch a tent in the campground.

She didn't seem to be the camping type. Her possessions showed a consistent bias toward luxury, prestigious names, and costliness. The minuscule closet was packed with cloth-ing, the labels a virtual catalog of exclusive shops from Los Angeles to Paris. She seemed to have a penchant for high, wedge-soled shoes; there were four pairs. One was caked with mud. He recognized the ripple-patterned sole from the track he'd found behind Reub's cabin.

That was only confirmation of an assumption and didn't surprise him. Neither did the revelation that Mrs. Bonnet was not a natural blonde, that she wore a wig. One of the three pieces of matched leather luggage was a wig box. The hairs caught in the brush on the dresser were red. However, close examination disclosed that she wasn't a natural redhead, ei-ther; the roots were gray. But Conan was quite sure she *had* been a natural redhead.

A dresser drawer served as a storage place for three purses, and in one of them he found a driver's license, which in-formed him that she was 5 feet, 3 inches tall, weighed 114 pounds, had brown eyes, and was sixty years old, but still— as the photograph attested—steadfastly redhaired.

The purse contained another interesting item: a small .22 automatic, the type known as a Saturday night special. It was fully loaded, but hadn't been cleaned since it was last fired.

A leather folder of business cards offered enlightenment about her name. Mimi Bonnet was president of Dwight Bon-net Real Estate, Inc.—"Established 1936"—in Los Angeles. Apparently, Dwight was, or perhaps—since Mimi was now president—had been the Mr. that went with Mrs. Bonnet.

Conan checked the luggage and found nothing startling

except a box of .22 cartridges for the gun. It occurred to him
that she might have the one object for which he was searching
with her; she always carried a large camera bag on her pho-
tographic sojourns. Interesting, he thought absently, that
there was not one roll of film, exposed or otherwise, nor any
informational notes in this room. Did she keep that in the
camera bag, too? Or had she even bothered to load the camera?

He went to the window to look out into the street; he'd
been in the room ten minutes and felt his time running out.
Then he stood looking around the room, his frustration
mounting until his gaze stopped at the small table by the bed
on which a kerosene lamp, an ashtray, and a Gideon Bible
rested. He hesitated, then with a faint smile reached for the
Bible. Two pieces of paper were inserted in it as if marking
a place. It was Exodus 20. One of the sheets was a clipping
of a newspaper article that had appeared in the Los Angeles
Times the day after the Owyhee County coroner's jury
reached its verdict on the death of Lee Langtry. Obviously,
the AP correspondent who picked up the story thought the
discovery of a skeleton in a ghost-town mine tunnel quaint.

The other sheet was folded double, and Conan handled it
with care; the paper was fragile with age. One corner was
missing. The tiny scrap in Reub's box would fit nicely there,
and the faint impressions in the paper would also make a nice
fit with the .38, proof that this paper had lain under that gun
for a long time. That he could test, and did.

Satisfied with the results, he unfolded the sheet, which was
about half the size of regulation typewriter paper and had
probably come from a memo pad. The Lang-Star Mining
Company logo was printed at the top, and the message was
written in a large, sharply angled hand.

Amanda—
There has been a HITCH. We'll have to change our plans.
The keys are in the car—take it and get out of here now.
I'll meet you in Reno.
                                                    Lee

Conan frowned, wondering about the terse, nearly formal tone—no terms of endearment, no "Mimi"—and about the capitalization of the word "hitch."

Then with a glance at his watch, he folded the note and slipped it into his shirt pocket. He didn't usually sink to larceny when conducting an unlawful search, but if this needed rationalization, he could assure himself that he was simply recovering stolen property. Of course, it was very doubtful that he would ever return it to Reub. And he wondered how it had come into Reub's possession.

As he descended the stairs, he heard the ringing of the front door bells, but to his relief they only heralded the arrival of a family of sightseers. When he passed through the lobby, he nodded to them, then set the bells ringing again as he stepped out onto the porch. John and Bill were gone, he noted, and so was Reub Sickle's jeep.

Conan walked south, pausing as he passed the white Cadillac to look behind him, and he saw Mimi Bonnet approaching the hotel down the road from the north. She was a long way from Long Gulch, which wasn't odd in itself, but he wondered where she had been. To the old powder houses, perhaps. Or the cemetery. The latter seemed more likely.

CHAPTER 14

The generator was off for the night, and the fireplace, where Delia was busy rearranging a crackling blaze, offered a warm light augmented by the fainter fires of two kerosene lamps.

"Delia, you're a born mother hen," Conan said from the comfortable depths of the wing chair where he was ensconced with an ice pack to comfort his aching head and a glass of straight Waterfill & Frazier. Another delectable meal was behind him—or rather, within him—and the silent mountain night held sway beyond the windows.

Delia laughed as she put aside the poker and sat down on the couch. "Good thing I have some chicks to mother-hen occasionally. How are you feeling, Conan? I mean honestly."

"There you go—mother-henning again. Do you consider Clare one of your chicks?"

She glanced unconsciously upward toward Clare's bedroom. "Yes, I suppose so, but it's not a one-way street, you know. I need Clare as much as she needs me, although most folks don't understand that. My daughter, Kathleen—she's the one who lives down near Nyssa; her husband has a farm there—she keeps telling me Clare should be in a nursing home where somebody could keep an eye on her all the time.'' Delia smiled tolerantly, her clear gray eyes delving into the flames. ''What Kathy doesn't understand is that if they put Clare in a nursing home, they'll have to put *me* in one, too.''

Conan frowned and sipped at his bourbon. ''I hope it never comes to that. You don't belong in a nursing home.''

She studied him, still smiling. ''Who does? Nobody goes to a place like that because they want to. But it may come to that. Old age is as much a part of life as death is.''

She made that statement casually but not lightly, and Conan was silenced by it. After a moment, she turned again to the fire, its amber light burnishing the lined planes of her face. ''Everything has its seasons; beginnings and endings, and there's no way around them. I guess maybe there shouldn't be. There's a reason for all of it, even if we can't understand it.'' Then she took a long breath as she looked around at Conan. ''And that's enough of that subject. Conan, what about . . . I mean—''

''Am I any closer to finding out who killed Lee? Well, I suppose I am in a way. At least, I have a great deal more information than I did three days ago.''

''Does all that information add up to anything?''

He hesitated, frowning into the fire. ''If it does, I haven't been able to make sense of the total. All I can offer now is speculation.''

She crossed her arms, shoulders hunched as if she felt a chill. ''Do you have any speculations about what's been happening to Clare? Why would anybody want to frighten her like that? She won't even go to her grove now unless I go with her. And searching her room—I just don't understand.''

''Neither do I. Not entirely. It *is* related to the murder, though. Delia, is this investigation turning out to be more than you bargained for?''

She smiled crookedly. ''Quite a bit more, but I'm not ready to call it quits, if that's what you mean.''

''I'm glad to hear that.'' He put his glass on the side table and rose. ''There's something I'd like to ask you about. It's up in my room. I'll get it.''

Delia only watched him curiously as he left the parlor, and when he returned a few minutes later, she apparently hadn't moved. He handed her the gun he'd found in Reub's cabin, pointing out the scratched initials. "I think this probably belonged to Lee. Do you know anything about it?"

She turned the weapon over in her hands and asked absently, "Where did you find this thing?"

"Is it Lee's?"

"Yes." She returned it to Conan. "I think so, anyway. I remember he had a gun like this he kept at home. He said he was away so much, and that meant Clare was alone a lot. He thought she should have a gun handy." Then with a bitter laugh, "That was when they were first married. Later on, he didn't seem to care whether she was alone or not."

Conan nodded as he sank into his chair and put the gun on the side table. "Have you any idea where it might have been at the time of the murder?"

"Oh, Lord, no idea at all. I can ask Clare if she remembers."

There was a questioning inflection in that, and after a moment Conan nodded. "Ask her, if the opportunity arises. Delia, have you talked to her at all about the murder?"

A sigh escaped her. "I tried, and so did Andy Newbolt, but she won't even believe Lee's dead half the time, and the rest of the time . . . well, she can't talk about it."

"And Dex Adler? Would he talk about it to you?"

She eyed Conan sharply. "What would he say about it? I mean, that he hadn't already said forty years ago?"

"That's what I'd like to know."

"Oh, Conan, I know Dex has been awfully cantankerous about this whole thing, but he really means well."

"I hope so. Does he believe Tom was guilty?"

"No, of course not. At least . . ." She paused, clasping her hands around her knees. "I don't know. Maybe he says he thinks Tom is innocent just for my sake. Mostly, I don't think it matters to him who's guilty."

"I'd say it matters—*something* matters a great deal to him. Still waters run deep."

Delia regarded him with an inquiring half-smile. "What was that?"

"Something Lettie said about Dex. I have the feeling she'd like to cast Dex as the villain of this piece."

Delia was visibly shocked, then doubtful. "Are you sure? I always thought Lettie and Dex got along fine. They worked in the same office for a long time, you know."

But proximity seldom breeds respect. Conan didn't pursue that, however. "Delia, do you have a sample of Lee's handwriting?"

"*Lee's* handwriting? Well, I don't know. Clare probably has. . . ." Then she rose and crossed to the bookshelves. "Maybe there's something here. Bring that lamp, would you?"

Conan brought the lamp from the table and held it while she went down the rows of books. She pulled three out and looked inside the covers, but put them back. "Some of these were Lee's," she explained, pulling out another: *Handbook for Prospectors and Operators of Small Mines*, by M. W. von Bernewitz. "Here it is. He put his name in this one."

Conan took the book. Inside the front cover Lee had written, "Leland Langtry—Silver City." A scant sample, but for Conan's purpose it was enough.

"Thanks, Delia. Do you mind if I take this upstairs with me?"

"You're welcome to it." She was on the verge of a question, but Conan turned away and put the lamp on the table, then picked up his whiskey glass.

"I'll finish this upstairs, too."

She nodded acceptance both of that statement and the termination of the discussion. "Good idea for you to get to bed early. You've had a hard day. Oh—you need some more aspirin?"

He laughed. "Thank you, yes. It *has* been a hard day, but I'm lucky to be so hardheaded."

Conan readied himself for bed, downed four more aspirin, then took the note he'd purloined from Mimi Bonnet's room out of his briefcase, carefully opened it on the bed, and by the light of a kerosene lamp, compared it to the handwriting in Lee's book.

The result of that examination wouldn't stand in court—he didn't pretend to be a handwriting expert—but it left no doubt in his mind. Lee Langtry *had* written this note. But when and where? And more important, why?

Lee was forty years past answering those questions, and Reub Sickle, who had safeguarded this message for the same length of time, wasn't even admitting it existed; not to Conan. And Amanda Count, to whom Lee had addressed it—

The Roseberrys had been right. Clare had seen a ghost yesterday at their store: the ghost of Amanda Count reincarnated as Mimi Bonnet.

Amanda/Mimi no doubt knew the answers to Conan's questions. He put the note back into his briefcase, then climbed into bed, groaning as he sought a comfortable place to lay his aching head.

It had, indeed, been a hard day.

CHAPTER 15

Conan was late—at least, by the standards of the house—in waking. It was nine o'clock before he left his bed. But sleep had been elusive last night. While he dressed, he heard voices from downstairs, one a man's. He went out on the balcony in time to see Vern Roseberry departing, swinging jauntily down the road, despite his girth. When Conan descended to the kitchen, Delia and Clare were at the table delightedly sorting through a flat of fresh strawberries.

Clare smiled at him. "Look, Mr. Flagg—aren't they beautiful! Vern's son brought him three flats from the valley, so he gave us one. Oh, we'll have plenty of strawberry jam *this* winter."

Delia added, "And you'll have strawberries and cream this morning, Conan. Come on, Clare, you can start washing these while I fix Conan's breakfast."

Conan stayed out of the way by the hall door, noting Delia's practiced efficiency as she readied a colander, bowls, and sugar cannister for Clare by the sink. In contrast, Clare seemed confused and uncertain. That was underscored when she dropped the paring knife Delia handed her, tried to catch it, and cut her palm.

120

"Oh! Oh—I . . . Delia!" She stared wide-eyed at her hand, shakily rubbed the other across it, and with that succeeded in smearing both palms with blood. "Delia!"

Delia sighed and turned on the faucet, then held Clare's hands under the cold stream. "There, you see, it's just a little cut. Clare, for heaven's sake, there's nothing to cry about."

But she *was* crying, almost silently, head bowed. Delia gently dried her hands with a towel, then took a box of bandages from a cupboard. "I know, dear, it startled you. Let me put a Band-Aid on it. Now—that'll stop the bleeding. Oh—" She seemed momentarily chagrined. "Do you know what I forgot? The peas. I forgot to water them yesterday, and they really should have some water this morning before it gets too hot. Would you mind, Clare?"

She smiled wanly and nodded. "I'll take care of it. My gloves . . . my garden gloves . . ."

"I think you left them on the porch."

"Oh. Thank you . . ."

When the back door closed behind her, Delia picked up the knife, put it in the sink, then stood frowning out the window. "Clare had a bad night again. Nightmares." She looked around at Conan. "Maybe Dex was right: it's just damnfoolishness. All this raking over the coals of the past. Clare's worse than I've seen her for a long time. Like the crying; that's the second time this morning."

Conan got a mug out of a cupboard, then crossed to the stove and filled it from the coffee pot. "Delia, you can always call a halt to the investigation. You know that."

She hesitated before shrugging that off. "I told you last night, I'm not ready to wave any white flags yet. By the way, how's your head?"

"Better. The swelling's gone down."

"Good. Well, I'll get your breakfast started."

Conan sat down at the table and lit a cigarette, while she went to the stove and filled the firebox, squinting into the heat as the fire took hold. "Conan, I asked Clare about that gun you showed me. That's the other time this morning she started crying."

"I'm sorry. Could she tell you anything about it?"

"Well, she *did* remember that Lee kept a revolver at the house, but she didn't know what happened to it. She thought it was probably sold with the furniture and things. It all went to a second-hand dealer in Homedale." She closed the firebox and straightened. "That's what started the crying, talking about selling the house. She said, 'What will *Lee* think?' And she was right there in the cemetery when we buried him last month."

"In the Silver City cemetery?"

"Yes. The one across Jordan Creek as you come into town." She pulled a frying pan from the back of the stove to the front, then returned to the counter and began slicing a slab of bacon. "Conan, where *did* you find that gun?"

He took a drag on his cigarette. "In Reub Sickle's cabin."

She stopped in mid-slice, head coming around abruptly. "In *Reub's* cabin? How on earth did he get hold of it?"

"That's a good question."

"Well, what did he say?"

Conan laughed. "Nothing that bears repeating in polite company."

Her eyes narrowed. "How did you come to find it in Reub's cabin?"

"Well, that's something that probably doesn't bear repeating in polite company, either."

She mulled that, then resumed her slicing. "You think that gun fits into the murder somehow?"

"Probably, but I don't know how. Delia, are Reub and Dex Adler good friends?"

She raised an eyebrow, then took the bacon slices to the stove and slapped them into the skillet; they sizzled noisily, sending up a white, aromatic cloud. "I guess you'd say Dex and Reub are friends. Don't usually see much of each other, though. I wouldn't call them good friends; I mean, not *close* friends. Why?"

"I was just curious."

She eyed him obliquely, then laughed. "Of course. Just curious."

* * *

When Conan left the house he had no particular destination in mind, nor any purpose. The sky was curdled with a thin skim of clouds, the wind shifting uncertainly to the southwest. He guessed another storm was on its way. When he reached Morning Star Street, he turned right and walked up to the church, which was quite literally built on a rock: an outcropping of exfoliated granite. It was boarded up, although Delia had told him services were still occasionally held there. Not this Sunday, apparently. He retraced his steps down Morning Star, waved to Lettie Burbage, who was peering out of her second-story observation post. He rounded the bend in the road to the bridge, where he spent some time watching small fish darting in the refracted net of sunlight, then up to Washington Street to examine the ruins of the courthouse. At the back he found a series of small, windowless rooms that would have been underground before the collapse of the walls. He wondered if they had been jail cells. And he wondered where the staircase sandwiched between the courthouse and the next building to the south had originally led. Now it mounted into nothing but clear air.

Finally, as he turned east down Avalanche Avenue toward the Idaho Hotel, he wondered if he wasn't unconsciously searching for Mimi Bonnet. Sooner or later he would have to talk to her.

Then he saw the jeep parked between the hotel and the store. It was Reub Sickle's. But Reub was nowhere in evidence. Laurie Franklin was in the street near the jeep playing boisterously with Sheba, who ran in mad circles around her, laughing, it seemed, amid mock growls and exuberant barks. Conan watched Laurie, thinking of youth; age seemed to have been so much a part of his thoughts lately. Laurie, as blithely exuberant as Sheba, wore denim cut-offs and a sleeveless blouse, showing off long, golden limbs enhanced by the sun. She was a thing of beauty, and it seemed an insupportable tragedy that she would one day, inevitably, grow less golden, less supple, less tolerant of the dessicating power of the sun; that she would grow old.

Sheba was the first to see Conan—or perhaps to catch his

scent—and her playful barks turned serious. Sheba obviously never forgot or forgave.

Laurie, nonplussed at Sheba's sudden change of attitude, looked around at Conan, pushing her tawny hair back over her shoulder. "Oh, hello, Mr. Flagg." She knelt and stroked Sheba's head, and the dog was reassured enough to stop barking, but still suspicious. Laurie laughed up at Conan. "Don't worry about her. I don't think she bites."

He smiled, stopping a short distance away. "I hope you're right." They discussed the dog for a few minutes, then her owner, and Conan asked, "Where *is* Reub?"

Laurie rose and looked back toward the store. "Well, I suppose he's talking with the Roseberrys. I just came outside. Haven't seen him yet."

Conan nodded. "Have you seen Mrs. Bonnet?"

"Not since breakfast. She went out early this morning. Said it's her last day in Silver, and her last chance to get some more pictures." Laurie hesitated, turning sober, then, "Mr. Flagg, is . . . is Clare all right?"

"Well, all things considered, yes, I suppose she is."

"I hope so. I saw her yesterday evening. John and I were walking over near Slaughterhouse Gulch, and we ran into Clare and Delia. Clare seemed . . . funny, you know. She didn't even recognize us."

"She probably will next time she sees you." Laurie couldn't seem to make sense of that, but Conan didn't try to clarify it. He smiled and turned north up Jordan Street. "I'll see you later, Laurie." Sheba heralded his departure with another spate of barking.

He strolled past the hotel, noting the slatted shadows of the railings, but when he reached the north corner, he stopped. Between the wall of the hotel and the next building, there was an open space about ten feet wide, and through it he could see across Jordan Creek to Morning Star Street and the schoolhouse. He stopped to study that view because he saw someone walking north on Morning Star. Even from this distance, he had no trouble recognizing Reub Sickle.

Conan walked on past the building, a two-story hulk with all its windows boarded up. Beyond it, the street sloped down to Jordan Creek as it curved west briefly before resuming its northerly course, but before Conan reached the stream, he stopped and again looked across to Morning Star. There were two figures now, the second walking south. Dex Adler. When he met Reub, they talked for a few minutes, then Reub abruptly turned away and retraced his steps southward. Adler stood apparently undecided for a while, then followed him, but at a slow pace that suggested no attempt to catch up with him.

Interesting, Conan thought, then sighed resignedly when he heard a feminine voice calling his name. Betty Potter, rather an astonishing sight burdened and bristling with her equipment, was bearing down on him from the hotel.

"Good morning, Mr. Flagg. How goes the sleuthing?"

He managed a smile. "It's Sunday; a day of rest. I'm just sight-seeing. How goes the painting?"

She frowned up at the sky. "Oh marvelously, but I hate to see those clouds. They *do* spoil the light. I hope it's not going to rain again. I have to leave tomorrow."

"Monday seems to be the great day of exodus. Where are you working today?"

"The first powder house. Terrific walls. I'm trying acrylic on that. Where are you off to?"

Conan saw a wooden sign across the street with "Cemetery" incised over an arrow pointed westward and decided "I'm going to take a look at the cemetery."

"Oh, yes, I did a couple of watercolors there. Just *charming*! Well, I'd better hurry before the light goes. Have a good day!"

He watched her rattling along her way, shook his head, then crossed to the road the sign indicated. It followed the curve of Jordan Creek along an avenue of willows that put him out of sight of Mrs. Potter within a short distance. He might have changed his mind then, but the cemetery seemed as good a destination as any. The road petered out when it reached the foot of the open slope where the cemetery lay exposed to the sun but surrounded by aspen and fir. It was fenced with metal poles suspended between stone posts, the untended grounds given over to low-lying thickets of weeds with lupine and balsam providing the only color.

Conan wandered the paths between the graves, thinking of the poets who had found their substance in places like this where life and death were juxtaposed and the fey evanescence of individual lives was so inescapable. Many of the markers were simple wooden planks blasted to the grain by sun and ice, names and dates obliterated. Some graves were marked only by small metal tablets bearing the poignant designation "Unknown." Others, however, were marked more permanently with polished stone. White marble seemed to have been the material of choice in this land of granite mountains. A few plots were enclosed in elaborate, wrought-iron fences. He paused by one in which young aspen grew, crowding as they shaded the stones. There was—typically for old cemeteries—a tendency to a particular style of marker. Here truncated obelisks had been popular either with the bereaved or the stonemasons. An incised drape was a frequent decorative motif, as were scrolls and open books.

He noted the number of children's graves, like the two infant daughters of A. A. and S. B. Getchell, whose brief lives were memorialized with carved forget-me-nots. Nannie Frances, beloved daughter of Frank and Hannah Hunt, born October 20, 1879, died October 25, 1880: "Our darling has gone to rest." Alice, only daughter of John and Christina Wagener, born August 19, 1885, died December 8, 1898. Frederick Julius, son of J.M. and Anna Brunzell, died March 25, 1877, "aged 11 yrs 2 mos 16 d's." For young Frederick, the stonemason added an optimistic verse:

> Gone to a land of pure delight
> Where saints immortal reign;
> Infinite day excludes the night,
> And pleasure banishes pain.

The survivors of Alfred Hicks, who died in 1896 at the age of forty-three, were equally optimistic—and affluent enough to mark his final resting place with a white marble monument over six feet high topped by a draped urn resting on an open book.

> 'Twill recompense the woes of earth
> To think we'll dwell with him in heaven.

But the parents of Lewis F. Leonard had apparently not been at all optimistic when they ordered the monument for their son, who died in 1887 at the age of nineteen. It was an imposing marker, again of white marble, employing the truncated obelisk form. It also used the motif of the book carved in full relief atop the shaft, but his book was irrevocably closed, and the poem incised on the back of the stone had Conan leaning closer for a second reading.

> Leaves have then time to fall,
> And flowers to wither at the north wind's breath,
> And stars to set; but all—
> Thou hast all seasons for thine own, O Death!

After a third reading, Conan took a deep breath, thinking of the Leonards' grief, wondering what young Lewis, at nineteen, had been like. Very much like John Kulik, no doubt, or golden Laurie Franklin.

But Lewis wasn't forgotten, even now. There was a coffee can wrapped in foil and filled with plastic flowers at the base of the stone. Similar plastic offerings lay at the feet of other monuments.

A short distance up the slope from Lewis's grave was another that attracted Conan's attention not because the marker was so unusual—it was an austere slab of red granite—but because the recently-turned earth indicated it was a new grave. There were no flowers on this grave, not even an uninvited wild flower, and no carving on the stone, nor poetry; nothing but the words, "Leland Langtry February 2, 1898—September 22, 1940." At least, Lee Langtry's existence was substantiated by this spare monument, but little more.

Conan continued upslope, pausing again when he reached

a weathered board streaked with blood-red rust stains from the nails securing the supports on its back. The legend was still legible, and in simple, block letters asserted that this marker was erected "In memory of Chris Studer, killed by Indians June 8th at South Mountain."

A little further up the slope, Conan came to a wrought-iron fenced plot that was better tended than the others; the weeds were cut back, and all the markers were intact and upright. The plot was dominated by a white marble obelisk on the front of which was carved an open book—that motif again—held by a disembodied hand, with an exquisitely sculpted rose rising from behind it. At the top of the monument was the name, "Starbuck." Seven Starbucks lay buried here, from Asa himself, to Thomas and ten-year-old Howard. Beneath the latter two markers, coffee-can vases held the dried husks of real flowers.

The sun burned hot through breaks in the clouds, and again the air had that typical prestorm oppressiveness. Conan walked on to the top of the cemetery where a Douglas fir offered an inviting span of shade, sat down on the ground with his back against one of the stone fence posts, and lit a cigarette. The view was dominated by the huge, dromedary hump of War Eagle Mountain. Even at its summit, there were tailings diminished by distance into flecks of white. A good part of Silver City was also visible to him: the Idaho Hotel; the church; the schoolhouse, where Lettie Burbage might well be looking out from her observation post toward the cemetery with her keen, birdlike eyes; the Starbuck house, where Delia and Clare were probably busy making strawberry jam for the winter to come; Dex Adler's house—and Conan wondered what Adler was doing at this moment.

He closed his eyes to listen to the sounds of bird cries, grasshoppers whirring from one sagebrush to the next, the surf sigh of wind in the fir boughs; the small subtleties that gave texture to the quiet. *Homo sapiens* was such an incredibly noisy animal; it seemed to fear silence as it feared darkness and had devoted much of its inventive energies to banishing both. Conan wondered why, when *Homo sapiens* was part and product of the largely silent natural world.

Perhaps because it was endowed with such pitifully inadequate ears. Conan opened his eyes and realized he was no longer alone in the cemetery, yet he had heard nothing to warn him of the arrival of another person here.

He started to rise, then stopped and smiled faintly.

Mrs. Bonnet, her camera and equipment case slung over one shoulder, was coming though the gate at the far end of the cemetery. As he watched, she walked purposefully toward the center of the cemetery, toward the one new grave. She didn't have to search for it, and that meant this wasn't her first visit here. She went directly to the grave where Leland Langtry was buried.

Apparently she didn't see Conan sitting motionless in the shadows of the fir. He moved slowly to put his cigarette out, still watching her. When she reached Lee's grave, she removed her sunglasses and stood gazing down at it. Finally, Conan rose and walked toward her. He had crossed half the distance between them before she became aware of him. She put on her sunglasses and walked away toward the gate. Conan quickened his pace. "Mrs. Bonnet . . ."

But she didn't pause or look around. He called out again. "Amanda!"

That stopped her. She seemed briefly transfixed, then she whirled around to face him. She didn't speak, however, only waiting silently until he stopped two paces from her, and even though she had to look up at him, he had the distinct feeling he was being looked down upon. There was a defiant lift in her half smile, but he saw nothing except his own reflection in her sunglasses.

The next move, apparently, was his. He took off his own glasses and put them in his shirt pocket, smiled amiably, and asked, "What does the word 'hitch' mean to you, Amanda?"

The lines of age around her eyes were briefly apparent. She said icily, "I understand you're a licensed private investigator, Mr. Flagg. Does that give you license to invade other people's privacy or to steal? And my name is Mimi Bonnet. *Mrs*. Mimi Bonnet."

"Forgive me, Mrs. Bonnet. As for invasion of privacy and

theft, I'm afraid you're not in a morally defensible position to complain about that. Perhaps Reub is, but you aren't.''

"Reub?" She laughed harshly. "How does he defend *his* morals?"

Conan hesitated, well aware that she was probing with that question; she wanted to know how much Reub had told him. He considered running a bluff, but decided against it; there was too much he didn't know.

Finally, he said, "I have no idea how Reub defends his morals. We aren't on friendly terms.''

"Oh? Well, Reub's rather hard to get on friendly terms with—or maybe you've noticed that?" Again, a cold laugh, then she asked impatiently, "What is it you want, Mr. Flagg?"

"First, I want to know about 'hitch'.''

"And second?"

He shrugged. "I want to know what happened at the Lang-Star office the night Lee Langtry was murdered.''

Her chin came up and there was a tremor of tension in her mouth, but she got that under control as she asked, "And third—or fourth? Come on, Mr. Flagg, let's get down to it.''

"To what?"

"To the price. Isn't that what this is all about? You've got something that by rights is mine, something you *stole* from me. But I'm not in a position to argue about that. The point is you've got it now, and, yes, I'm willing to pay for it. So, how much do you want?''

The bitterness of experience was in every word, and although Conan might under other circumstances have felt highly insulted, he didn't now. He said levelly, "You're making an error, Mrs. Bonnet. I have nothing for sale. All I want is the truth—nothing more—and I'm offering nothing in exchange.''

She seemed to consider that, head tilted slightly, then turned and walked to the low wall of stone surrounding one of the plots. She slipped the camera and case off her shoulder and seated herself on the wall, removed her sunglasses, then looked up at Conan. "Have you got a cigarette?''

He sat down beside her and provided the cigarette, then

lit it for her, thinking as he studied her face, unmasked finally, of the photograph in the missing persons file. Amanda
Count, ambitious child of poverty and abuse, her only birth-
right her beauty, still lived behind that face, but only in the
large, deep-set brown eyes. The contours of her face hadn't
been altered so much with age—she was still a vital and
attractive woman—but something had happened within her,
and the results were as effective as plastic surgery. She might
have dispensed with the blond wig to avoid recognition in
Silver City. All she needed was the dark glasses to hide the
eyes of Amanda Count.

She turned her head to blow out a stream of smoke, lips
curved in a cool smile. "So, Mr. Flagg, you're after the
truth, like Diogenes with his lamp."

Conan lit a cigarette for himself. "I think all Diogenes
was looking for was an honest man."

"Well, they're both hard to find. I still can't quite believe
there isn't something in this for you."

"Of course there is. A fee. I was hired to do a job. There's
also a matter of self-esteem."

She laughed at that. "Maybe *you're* that honest man. All
right, if all you're after is the truth, you can have it. At least,
the part of it I know."

"And there's nothing in it for you?"

"What would there be? Maybe I'm just tired of hiding."

He accepted that with a grain or two of salt. "Why did
you come out of hiding now? Why are you here?"

She looked toward the town. "Curiosity, I suppose. I read
an item in the *Times* about—well, you saw it. Forty years,
and I'd almost forgotten . . . no, I didn't forget; I couldn't
forget. But I'd made quite a success as Mrs. Mimi Bonnet.
Dwight—my husband—already had a good business built up
when I met him, and together we turned it into a big business, and since he died it's only gotten bigger. Anyway, it's
been enough to keep me busy, to keep me from thinking
about Lee and Silver City. Then I saw that article in the paper
and . . ." She closed her eyes briefly. "It all seemed to come
back on me. That's when I decided to come to Silver, to get
it out of my system."

Conan nodded. It was probably true, as far as it went. "And to get the note out of Reub's box?"

She called up a laugh. "Yes. That note didn't matter so much as long as no one knew Lee had been murdered, but when the body was found—well, I didn't feel easy about leaving it in Reub's hands. I mean, it placed me at the scene of the crime, and the way it was worded it could be interpreted as a brush-off. Lee had a reputation for disposing of his . . . women without much notice that way when he got tired of them. It gave me a motive for murder, if a jury wanted to interpret it that way, and I don't have much faith in an Owyhee County jury giving *me* the benefit of any doubt."

"But where does Reub come into this? How did he happen to have that note?"

She muttered sourly, "That dotty old bastard." Then with a sigh she leaned forward to rest her elbows on her knees. "All right, I'll tell you what happened the night Lee was murdered. That's what you want to know, isn't it?"

"I want to know who murdered Lee."

"Well, I can't tell you *that*."

He studied her doubtfully. "Can't or won't? Never mind, I'll take whatever you're willing to give me."

"A practical man, as well as honest. Look, it was all over by the time I got there. To the office, I mean. I was supposed to meet Lee there at nine o'clock that night, packed and ready to go. We were going to start a new life; new names, new *us*. It was . . . all very exciting."

"And this new life was to be financed with the Lang-Star payroll?"

She turned cold eyes on him. "It wasn't as if Lee didn't have a right to that money. He'd paid his dues over the years, and besides, when he and Tom Starbuck formed the partnership, Lee put up twenty thousand to buy into it. The mill was going to hell, but Tom wouldn't sell. Taking the payroll was the only way Lee could get out with something to show for his investment and nearly twenty years' work."

Conan only nodded, declining to pursue the ethics of Lee's timing or his willingness to leave a wife behind when he embarked on that new life. After a moment, Amanda's anger subsided, and she went on with her story.

"Well, I was a few minutes late getting to the office. Damn, that was a hard walk, me with two suitcases and five-inch heels." She smiled ruefully at that. "I still remember those shoes. Black patent, and the prettiest shoes I'd ever had on my feet. Anyway, when I got to the mill, there was a light in the office, and Lee's car was outside. I put my suitcases in the back seat, then went on in."

"The front door was unlocked?"

"Yes."

"Did you see anyone else?"

"*No.* Only . . . Lee." Something seemed to freeze behind her eyes. She took a long drag on her cigarette, then threw it down and ground it into the dirt with her heel. "He was on the floor in Tom's office."

Conan waited for her to go on, then finally had to ask, "He was dead?"

She winced, then nodded. "Yes."

"Would you . . . can you describe the position of the body?"

She could, after another pause. "He was lying face down with his right arm under him, and the knife . . . I guess he fell right on it."

Which would explain why the knife had been driven into the body so hard it cracked ribs—an explanation that didn't call for a strong man or an Amazon wielding it. "Did you notice whether he was wearing his wedding ring or a gold pocket watch?"

She smiled humorlessly at that. "He damn sure wasn't wearing his wedding ring *that* night. He never did when he was with me, anyway. The watch—and I know what watch you're talking about—I don't know whether he had it on him or not. I didn't . . . search the body."

Conan found himself reluctant to continue questioning her. Her grief was either genuine or she was an extraordinarily good actress. "What about the office? Any sign of a struggle—anything like that?"

"Oh, there'd been a struggle, all right. The place was a mess."

"Was the safe open?"

"Yes. And empty. There were a few papers still left in it, but you're thinking about the money—right? Well, it wasn't there. Neither was Lee's briefcase. That's where he would've put the money. I know that because when we were making our plans, he said he intended to leave Silver with 'a briefcase full of green.' *I* didn't take that money."

He smiled. "You're anticipating me. All right, what about the note and Reub?"

"The note was on the floor by the desk. I saw my name on it and picked it up, and that's when Reub walked in. His face—God, it was awful then. You know about his fight with Lee?"

"Yes, I heard about that."

"Meddling old fool, mooning all those years over Clare, but he never had the guts to do anything about it. Anyway, there he was in the door with his rifle pointed right at me. I thought he was going to kill me; I really did. He told me to give him the note, and he read it. Damn, I was surprised he even knew how to read. Then he said it looked like Lee was giving me the old heave-ho. He was the one who put that idea in my head, about that note giving me a motive and placing me at the scene of the crime. Wily bastard. I was so scared, with Lee lying there dead, and Reub waving that rifle in my face. He told me to take Lee's car and leave town and never come back. If I didn't leave, or if I ever tried to come back, he said he'd show that note to the sheriff and swear he saw *me* kill Lee because he was going to dump me. And what the hell did I have to stay in Silver for with Lee dead? I ran for the car and drove out of town so fast, it's a wonder I didn't end up in Jordan Creek."

Conan took a long drag on his cigarette, eyes slitted. "Then it was Reub who hid the body in the mine adit."

She shrugged indifferently. "I guess so. I didn't have the vaguest idea what happened after I left. It was five years before I even found out that nobody knew Lee'd been murdered."

"How did you find out? From your sister?"

"No. As far as Doris or anybody else in Idaho was concerned, I didn't exist. I didn't write home for news. I found out from the library in L.A. It took five years because when I first hit town, I was just a kid from the sticks. I didn't know libraries had newspaper files. Hell, my folks didn't even know libraries had *books*. Anyway, the main L.A. library had a file of *Idaho Statesman*s—the Boise paper. I found an item in the September twenty-fourth, nineteen-forty issue about the robbery in Silver. The *robbery*. That was all. No, it said something about the police looking for me—and *Lee*."

"So, you realized Reub had disposed of the body?"

"I didn't know what had happened, but I damn sure wasn't coming back to find out. Not then."

Conan paused over that, then: "You didn't go directly to Los Angeles. You drove to Reno, didn't you?"

She crossed her arms, rubbing them as if she were cold, then looked up at the sky. "It's going to rain again. Yes, I drove to Reno. That's where Lee and I had planned to go first. I didn't really think about where I was going, actually, and I don't remember anything about the drive. I just seemed to wake up about dawn, and there I was in Reno."

"Why did Lee schedule Reno as your first stop? To get a divorce from Clare?"

Amanda laughed curtly. "No way. Lee knew Tom would have the police after us because of the money, so there wouldn't be time for formalities like a divorce. The only reason he picked Reno was that he'd already made arrangements with a man there—his name was Otto Spicer." Her lips curled in disgust. "Filthy, slimy little man. Anyway, Otto was in the paper business. I told you Lee planned for us to start out with new names. Otto was going to supply us with the papers we needed—birth certificates, driver's licenses, that sort of thing. Well, when I realized where I was, it came through to me that I'd left a body behind—I didn't know then that nobody had found it—and an empty safe, so I decided I could use that new identity. We were going to be Mr. and Mrs. Christopher L. Studer, by the way. Christopher *Lee* and Mimi." She gestured toward the marker memorializing Chris Studer's death at the hands of Indians. "That's where Lee got the name." Briefly, she found that amusing, then her smile faded, the lines in her face emerging harshly. "I went to see Otto. Lee had already paid half his price for the papers; there was only two-hundred dollars owing. I had about three hundred with me, so I offered to pay the full two hundred for just one set of papers. But that son of a bitch knew he had me in a corner, damn him. *Four* hundred, he said. So, I started hitting the pawn shops with my luggage and Lee's and every piece of jewelry we had. I tried to sell the car, but nobody would touch it; I guess they figured it was too hot. God, I've never been through a night and a day like that. It was a taste of pure hell."

Conan waited through the silence that followed, reading in her face the gut-turning memories that forty years had only made more mordant. He had no doubt that this emotion, at least, was genuine. Finally, she began fumbling in her camera bag. "I've got some cigarettes in here somewhere."

He offered another of his, and she nodded her thanks when he lighted it. Then after inhaling deeply, she resumed her story. "I ended up with a few clothes in a paper sack and enough money to buy a bus ticket to Los Angeles, with twenty-seven dollars left over."

"Why Los Angeles?"

"I don't know. I guess I thought that's where the action was in those days." Then with a short laugh, "And maybe I was thinking about Hollywood—you know, getting discovered while sitting in a soda fountain wearing a tight sweater. Well, that idea didn't last long. Damn, I took any job I could get and lived anywhere I could find a cheap enough bed without too many fleas in it. But I never slept in anything but a *single* bed. Anyway, I finally landed a job in Dwight's office. He was a sweet guy and never been married, even if he wasn't exactly a young man. I figured I could do worse. It took a while, but I got him to the altar finally. Poor Dwight, he died ten years later. Heart attack."

"Did you have any children?"

"Hell, no. I didn't want any. I liked Dwight, but not enough to tie myself down with a bunch of runny-nosed kids." She gave Conan a slanted look. "You think that sounds hard, don't you? Well, I didn't love Dwight, but I can tell you this: he damn sure got his money's worth out of me. *Yes*, I'm hard. I learned *hard* right here in Owyhee County. I learned it from my father. You know, I never remember seeing him sober; not once. He was the kind of man who liked to knock his wife and kids around at least once a week; the kind of man who raped both his daughters. I was fourteen. That was the *first* time. Poor Doris was only twelve the first time. And my mother—she taught me about hard, too. She was thirty-seven the last time I saw her, and she looked sixty-seven. All she had was religion, and her God never forgave anybody anything. And I learned hard from the *good* people of Silver, all those proper, upstanding citizens—the ones who called me a tramp or a whore—and that's one thing I never was—the ones who turned the only beautiful thing that ever happened to me in my life into something ugly. Lee. Lee Langtry. He was . . . and then I lost that, too."

Again, Conan was silenced by the brute intensity of emotion, and again, he regarded it as genuine. He also found it frightening. If this were the tip of the iceberg—that part of her feelings she would expose to him—what was the submerged part of this iceberg like?

She apparently remembered her cigarette then and took a puff. "Well, I seem to be doing a lot of feeling sorry for myself. But you asked for it, Diogenes."

He laughed. "Yes, and I'm grateful for it."

"Are you? But skeptical?" Her smile was cool and ironic.

"I'm always skeptical. I still don't understand why you repossessed that note. Reub didn't bring it up during the inquest. What made you think he would later?"

"Because he's a dotty old man, and I don't trust him. And because it's *mine*. He had no right to even touch it."

"And you wanted no loose ends, nothing to tie you—or rather, Amanda Count—to Silver or the murder."

Something flickered in the dark shadows of her eyes, then she laughed. "I suppose so."

Conan hesitated, then, "Is there anything else you can—or will—tell me about the murder?"

"No. I've told you all I know about it."

He didn't voice his skepticism about that. "Did you see Lettie Burbage that night?"

Her eyes widened, then she broke out in a laugh. "What's that old biddy been telling you?"

"Oh, she's been quite informative," Conan replied evasively.

"I'll just bet she has. What an old maid. Yes, I know she was married. I always figured her husband probably died of sheer frustration."

"What *did* he die of?"

"Well, as a matter of fact, it was a mining accident."

"Did you see her that night?"

"I didn't see Lettie any more than was absolutely necessary at any time. Why?"

Conan didn't try to answer that. Amanda's lack of concern was revealing enough. If she'd seen anyone other than Reub at the scene of the murder, it wasn't Lettie Burbage. He asked, "Did you happen to see Dex Adler?"

"What are you doing—checking off suspects? Look, I told you everything I know about the murder."

"Yes, so you said. All right, do you know anything about a gun that belonged to Lee: a thirty-eight revolver." Then, seeing her eyes narrow slightly, he added, "Yes, the gun that was in Reub's box with the note."

"I didn't know it was Lee's."

"Did he have it with him the night he was killed?"

"I don't know. I didn't see it, if he did."

"Did you ever see him with it?"

She said irritably, "The first time I ever saw that gun was in Reub's box. I don't know anything about it."

Conan dropped that subject, but not because he was convinced of the truth of her answers; he simply recognized the futility of pursuing it further. And he was thinking of the third object in Reub's box.

"What about the cameo brooch?"

"I don't know anything about that, either. Maybe you should ask Reub." There was nothing subtle about the barb attached to that.

But he ignored it. "What does the word 'hitch' mean?"

He didn't succeed in catching her off guard. "I really don't have the foggiest idea." Then she tossed the cigarette away and rose. "And that's all the questions I'm going to answer. I've answered more than I should, anyway, considering who you're working for."

Conan came to his feet, too, startled by that apparent allusion to Delia. "What do you mean—who I'm working for?"

She said coldly, "I told you, I'm not answering any more questions, but I have one for you: What are you going to do with that note?"

"I don't know. I suppose I should give it to Andy Newbolt, but after so many years, and after going through so many hands, I'm not sure it has any value as evidence now."

She was silent for a moment, looking up at him with a calculating eye. Then: "So, why not give it to the one person who has a real right to it?"

"You? I can't do that, and you know it."

"Why the hell not?" she demanded angrily. "Who are you to decide what should be done with it?"

He sighed. "Amanda, I'm not—"

"Don't call me that! What do you want? Am I supposed to *beg* for it?"

"No! That's not the point. If anyone has a right to decide its disposal, it's the sheriff."

Her face went red, and at first she seemed too enraged to speak, then she burst out, "Give it to him, then! Go ahead! I'm not afraid any more, and if he has any questions, by God, I'll tell him more than he or anybody in this town *wants* to know! I've lived with this thing too long to give a damn now!"

"Ama—Mrs. Bonnet!" But she had picked up her camera and bag, and was stalking out of the cemetery.

Conan watched her until she was out of sight in the willows, feeling as if his ears were a little singed with that outburst. He didn't like the threat underlying it because he didn't understand it. But the volatile emotion behind it was clear enough.

Finally, he turned and walked slowly toward Lee Langtry's grave. He was looking at the terse words encompassing a man's life between two dates, when a conchoidal pockmark suddenly appeared in the polished granite. The sharp crack of the gun reverberated from one mountain to the next.

Conan hit the ground. Reflex. He wasn't even sure what had happened. Not until a second shot sent up a spurt of dirt only a foot from his head.

Rifle shots. Some part of his mind made that assessment, but it was only a peripheral awareness at the moment. Another fountain of dirt exploded near his head as he crawled across brittle sagebrush to a looming headstone and made himself as flat and small as possible against the north face of the stone. A singing crack—a bullet ricocheting off the south face. He spat out dust and weed fragments, wondering how long he would—or could—remain pinned down here until help arrived.

It was some time before he realized the fusillade had ceased. He lay panting, listening to the mountain silence over the pounding of his pulse in his ears; his head ached miserably. At length, he decided the moment of truth had come and cautiously looked around the stone.

He didn't end up with a bullet between his eyes, and with a heartfelt sigh of relief, he rested on his elbows while the tension sagged out of him, leaving him briefly spent.

It was young Lewis Leonard's memorial that had provided him protection. He stared at the words incised in the stone.

Thou hast all seasons for thine own, O Death!

CHAPTER 16

By the time Conan got to his feet and dusted himself off, anger had overwhelmed relief, and the shallow cut across his right hand—undoubtedly caused by a flying fragment of marble—only fed the anger. He scanned the thick growth of aspen bordering the cemetery on the south. The sniper had probably been hidden there, but a search would be futile. He'd be long gone by now.

Conan stormed out of the cemetery and up the willow-lined road into town, his jaw clenched painfully. This, he muttered to himself, was going too damned far. Those shots had been too close, and in that setting, with so many polished stone slabs to deflect the bullets, too potentially fatal to be shrugged off. When he reached the Idaho Hotel, Jake and John Kulik and Laurie Franklin were outside in the street, along with a few curious sightseers. Jake began asking anxious questions about the shots, but Conan didn't answer them. Reub Sickle was coming out of the hotel door, the ringing of its bells incongruously sweet.

Conan demanded, ''Where the hell have you been?''

Reub only scowled at him, head lowered, and it was Jake

Kulik who said, "He's been here. We were having a beer in the dining room."

Conan nodded and strode past them, ignoring the renewed spate of questions. Mimi Bonnet was standing on the porch by her car, and perhaps he imagined a faint, cold smile curling her lips. He didn't stop to explore the smile, but headed down the slope between the hotel and store, then across the clearing to Jordan Creek. He was breathing hard by the time he reached the schoolhouse but he didn't pause, and he totally ignored Lettie Burbage's shouted inquiry. Neither his pace nor his anger slackened as he climbed the road past the Starbuck house all the way to Dex Adler's. His footfalls thudded across the porch, and his fist went up to pound on the door.

"Adler!" More pounding; he didn't even feel the impacts. *"Adler!"*

The door flew open, and Adler stood staring at him. "What in God's name—"

"I've had enough of your games! I'm not leaving Silver until I've finished my job here, and I *will* finish it. That's a warning!"

Adler's face went red as he glowered from under his heavy brows. "I don't know what the hell you're talking about, Flagg."

"I'm talking about getting shot at, getting knocked out, and finding rattlers in my car! And I'm talking about Lee Langtry's murder—"

"Get out of here! Just get out, damn it!"

"Adler, I won't—" But whatever he *wouldn't* was cut off abruptly. Adler slammed the door in his face, and Conan heard the snap of a bolt sliding home.

"Damn." That was as much for himself as for Adler. His anger dissipated with a long exhalation, and he turned, shoulders sagging. That, he thought bitterly, was not the most intelligent move he'd made in this case.

But hadn't Adler seemed a little breathless, as if he'd just finished an uphill run? And his shoelaces had been untied. Was that because Conan had caught him in process of changing from another pair of shoes soaked during a hasty crossing of Jordan Creek near the cemetery?

Perhaps. It would be more pertinent to have a look at the rifles hung near Adler's fireplace, but obviously that was out of the question, unless Conan opted to break down the door. Then he would probably find himself staring down the barrel of one of those guns, while Adler called the sheriff and virtuously claimed he was defending his house and person from attack.

Conan sighed, noting as he crossed the road that Delia and Clare were looking out the north window of the parlor. When he went inside the house, they were in the hall, Delia only faintly bewildered, but Clare, to his surprise, trembling with anger, tears shining in her eyes.

"All you ever do is make *trouble*!" she declared accusingly. "Why don't you go away! I don't want you here, I don't want you—oh, just go *away*!" And with that, she burst into noisy sobs and stumbled up the stairs.

Delia took a deep breath, then followed her. "I'll be back, Conan."

Feeling much the worse for wear, he retreated to the bathroom at the end of the kitchen hall and washed his face and arms, ending with a dousing of cold water, then went to the kitchen. It was permeated with the heady scent of strawberries, and a row of rubescent pints was cooling on the counter. On the stove, more jam bubbled over the rim of a kettle. He found a potholder and shifted the kettle to the back of the stove, then seeing the coffee pot still warming there, he poured himself a mug and took it with him out on the front porch. There was still some shade and a fitful breeze to temper the noonday heat that heightened the perfume of lilacs. Thunderheads were massing behind Florida Mountain and Potosi Peak, but they seemed to be holding themselves in abeyance, as if awaiting some cosmic order to advance.

He had finished the coffee and two cigarettes when Delia joined him on the porch step. She brushed at the front of her apron; the ruffled bodice was spotted with red. "I never seem to be able to put up a batch of jam without getting it all over me. Well, what was that all about? With Dex, I mean."

Conan could laugh at it now. "Just a little flare of temper on my part."

"Looked like a pretty good flare. We . . . we heard gunshots earlier."

"They were aimed at me. That's what ignited my temper."

"Oh, dear." She frowned, then, "You think it was *Dex* who shot at you?"

"Did you see him around his house in the last half hour?"

She shrugged uncomfortably. "No, but Clare and I were back in the kitchen. At least, till we heard you shouting for Dex. But, Conan, why would he want to shoot at you?"

"Yes, why would he? Delia, I must have the truth—and I think you know it—about Dex's opportune financial windfall. The one that occurred right after the murder and robbery."

She folded her hands in her lap, frowning down at them. "Conan, it doesn't have anything to do with Lee or the robbery."

"Good. But I still want to know about it."

And she still hesitated. Then, with a sigh of resignation, she said, "I gave my word I'd never tell anybody. I'll have to have your word on that, too."

He was beginning to feel another flare of temper approaching ignition point, but only nodded and said, "Delia, if it doesn't have anything to do with Lee or the robbery, you have my word I won't discuss it with anyone."

That satisfied her. "Well, Dex *was* in a lot of trouble financially just before the robbery. He was about to lose all the property he'd invested in for want of a few thousand dollars to keep up the payments. But he's a proud man. I'd never have known about it if Irene hadn't come to me. Well, I had some money of my own. It was willed to me by my grandfather, and Tom always insisted I keep it in a separate account. It was to be my own nest egg. Even when the mill went bankrupt, Tom wouldn't touch that money. Anyway, when Irene told me about Dex's problems, I offered to loan him the money he needed out of that account. He agreed to it, but I don't think he would have if Irene hadn't begged him to, and he'd only accept it if I promised never to tell anybody about it. And I didn't until now; not even Tom.''

Conan rested his elbows on his knees, and he had a feeling that what she was about to tell him would not contribute to the solution of this case. ''When was the loan made?''

''Well, we made the arrangements about a week before the murder, but it was that night when the actual transaction took place. I'd gotten the money out of the bank in Homedale in cash, and Dex came over that night to pick it up. Tom was in the parlor working, like I told you, so Dex came around the back to the kitchen.''

Conan nodded. ''What time?''

''About eight thirty-five. He was telling the truth when he said he saw Lee drive up to the office at eight-thirty. He just didn't explain that he was on his way over to our house then. That's why he happened to be out on his porch.''

''When did he leave your house?''

''It wasn't until nine-thirty at least. Dex needed somebody to talk to once in a while, and—well, I guess he always felt he could depend on me.''

''Yes, I can understand that. I wish I could verify that eight-thirty departure time for Lee.''

''Well, Clare says that's when he left, too. I mean, she said that right after the robbery when the sheriff questioned her, and she didn't know then what Dex had said about the time.''

''They were questioned separately?''

''Yes. Dex stayed up at the office with Tom until Sheriff Kenny got there. Lathe went there first, then he came to Clare's house to talk to her. I was with her. In fact, I remember *after* she told Lathe what time Lee left, he said something about Dex seeing him go, too, at the same time.''

Conan's breath came out in a long sigh. ''Dex is a fortunate man. You've not only deprived him of a motive but given him an alibi.''

''I told you not to worry about Dex. I'm sorry I didn't feel like I should tell you why before.''

''That's all right, Delia.'' Then his hands clenched and opened. ''But, damn it, why is he so averse to an investigation? Why is he making life so difficult—not to speak of dangerous—for me?''

Delia caught her breath. ''You don't really think he had anything to do with what's happened to you? Conan, he was over at his house yesterday when you got that bump on your head.''

''I think he had a great deal to do with what's happened to me—especially today—but he hasn't been working alone.''

''Who's he working with? Reub?''

Conan looked at her sharply. ''What makes you say that?''

''Just the questions you've been asking lately.''

''Oh. Well, yes, I think Reub is his partner.''

''But, why? What do either one of them have to hide?''

''Rhetorical questions seem to be *my* department lately. Don't you start with them.''

She took a handkerchief from her apron pocket and pressed it to her brow. ''Oh, it's hot. If it's going to rain, I wish it'd get on with it. All right, Conan, I'll leave the questions to you. I just hope . . .'' She didn't finish that.

After a moment, Conan asked, ''You hope what?''

''I don't know.'' Then she rose, and she seemed uncharacteristically stiff and slow about it. ''It's about time for lunch. Maybe a sandwich and some iced tea. Does that sound good to you?''

Conan rose, too, but shook his head absently. ''Thanks, but I'm not really hungry. I think I'll take a walk.''

She nodded and watched him as he wandered off westward, hands thrust in his pockets, head bowed.

CHAPTER 17

It was a triple-shafted dolmen built not of stone but of massive, wooden beams studded with rusted bolts. Spanning the shafts beneath the horizontal beam was a thick camshaft, and affixed to one end of it, a wooden wheel at least six feet in diameter. Conan looked down on this enigmatic construction from a point slightly above it on the slopes of Potosi Peak, wondering what its function had been. All he knew was that it had been part of the Potosi mill that once occupied the site. It seemed ancient and mysterious, a relic of an undeciphered Stonehenge.

Many of the photographs he had seen of Silver City were taken from Potosi Peak, and it was a good vantage point; the whole of the town lay below him like an archeological site in process of excavation and restoration. He had come here unconciously, perhaps, in search of perspective, and certainly he had found that; at least, in a visual sense.

But he was seeking perspective on a construction of a far more intangible nature, one whose components were events and human emotions.

Adler's innocence was one component. That had to be accepted as a basic component now. Yet Adler was bent on thwarting Conan's investigation. The obvious motive for that was a desperate desire to protect someone, and if not himself, who else?

Lettie Burbage? Not if Adler felt for her a fraction of the animosity she betrayed for him when she presented him to Conan as a prime suspect. She had never been high on Conan's suspect list, but she was eliminated entirely now.

Reub Sickle, with whom Adler had formed a partnership of sorts? According to Delia, Adler and Reub weren't close friends. Would Adler join a conspiracy to protect Reub?

Still, Reub couldn't be eliminated from the suspect list. He had ample motive, and Amanda placed him at the scene of the crime. Not that Conan accepted her testimony at face value, but he accepted Reub's presence at the scene because of the note. ''The keys are in the car—take it and get out of here now.'' That implied that the note was written at the mill office—where the car was, and where Lee was expecting Amanda, to whom it was addressed—and it could only have been written in the short time between Lee's arrival at the office and his murder. Since Reub had the note in his possession, that meant he'd been in the office at about that time. Certainly he'd been there before Amanda departed, or she would have taken the note with her.

Conan walked to the top of a snowy mound of tailings; there was a green cast to the rock, and myriad mica sparks flashed under his feet. He found himself a suitable boulder to sit on and lit a cigarette. The wind plucked the smoke away toward Silver.

So, how would the scenario play if Reub were the killer?

It was probably on one of his nocturnal sojourns into town—which the Roseberrys indicated had been frequent during the month preceding the murder—that Reub saw Lee drive from his house to the office, followed him there, and watched through the window while Lee looted the Lang-Star safe. Then, full of righteous outrage, Reub stormed into the office, he and Lee argued—violently, to explain the signs of struggle—and Reub stabbed Lee with Tom's knife. Immediately afterward, Amanda appeared. Reub frightened her into making a hasty exit, then straightened up the office, and carried the body to the mine adit.

Conan took a drag on his cigarette, grimacing irritably, but not at the taste of the tobacco. That scenario didn't explain why Lee wrote the note, or what happened to the money. Of course, Amanda might have taken it, but Conan doubted that not only because he found her story about her hellish tour of Reno's pawn shops convincing, but because it was highly unlikely that Reub, after commandeering the note, would let her escape with that briefcase full of green.

If Amanda didn't take the money, did Reub? If so, what did he do with it? It hadn't been in his cabin, but that wasn't conclusive. He might have buried it somewhere, or tossed it in another abandoned mine adit, or even, conceivably, have deposited it in his own rather impressive—according to Vern Roseberry—bank account. But why would Reub take the money? He didn't seem to be at all interested in money *per se*, and he'd be well aware what a disaster the loss of that payroll would be to Tom Starbuck against whom he apparently had no grievance.

That, however, wasn't the factor that bothered Conan most in casting Reub as the killer. The murder weapon. Why would Reub use the knife when he undoubtedly entered the office with his ever-present rifle at ready?

The revolver. Conan rose and walked to the edge of the tailings, looking down the rubbled slope to Long Gulch Creek, its course marked by thickets of willows and young cottonwoods. But what his eyes were seeing wasn't registering in his brain.

He was thinking about Lee's gun; perhaps it entered the action here. If Lee had it with him that night, he probably wouldn't have had a chance to make use of it—not against Reub's rifle. But if Lee had previously given it to Amanda, if she arrived just after Reub—

Conan sighed. In that case, Reub would probably have been the victim, not Lee, or at least there would have been a shoot-out in the office that would have attracted everyone within hearing distance, and in these mountains and at that time, that would have been a lot of people.

And the note—it was still unexplained.

So, try another scenario. This time cast Amanda in the role of killer.

Amanda had said she was afraid the note might be interpreted as a brush-off, that Lee had a habit of discarding his women abruptly when he tired of them. Perhaps he did in fact mean to discard her, and perhaps he had a double motive in writing the note: to rid himself of Amanda *and* to send her off on a fool's errand to Reno, then make her the scapegoat for the robbery, while he headed in another direction with the money.

In what? Conan threw his cigarette down and crushed it under his heel. How did Lee plan to get out of town with the money if he sent Amanda off in his car? Well, possibly he planned to steal someone else's car. If he were morally capable of robbing his partner, he probably wouldn't balk at car theft.

At any rate, assume Lee planned to rid himself of Amanda in this fashion. It would certainly be imperative to the success of his plan that he be absent when she read the note. And assume she didn't arrive late for their assignation, as she claimed, but early, and found Lee in the office with the note. An argument ensued, which became violent, and Amanda, in self-defense, and with the proverbial fury of a woman scorned, stabbed Lee with the knife she found handy on the desk.

At this point, Reub Sickle made his entrance, commandeered the note, sent Amanda off to Reno, then thoughtfully cleaned up the office for her and disposed of the body.

"Damn." Conan leaned down to pick up a blue-green pebble, examined it briefly, then tossed it down into the trees.

If Amanda were guilty and Reub knew it, why would he let her go, much less encourage her to do so, much *less* cover her tracks for her?

And Conan wasn't entirely satisfied with the hypothesis that Lee had betrayed Amanda or even planned to. Amanda's feelings for Lee were still intense after forty years. Would she feel so strongly if he had betrayed her? And would she return to Silver now if she had murdered him? More likely

she'd be laughing up her sleeve, safe in California as Mrs.
Mimi Bonnet, perfectly happy to let Tom Starbuck bear the
burden of blame posthumously.

Why had Amanda come back to Silver? A key question,
but he doubted he'd have an answer to that until he had answered the larger question: who killed Lee?

And did Amanda know the answer to that question? He
reviewed their conversation in the cemetery, and he was convinced she did know, despite her protestations of ignorance.

Conan returned to his boulder and lit another cigarette.
The note. He kept coming back to that. One thing that bothered him about it was its cold tone. If Lee had written it in
order to deceive Amanda, the intelligent approach would be
to make it as warm as possible, to fill it with endearments,
and certainly to address her by his pet name for her, Mimi.
The very coldness of the wording as he wrote it would be
enough to arouse her suspicions. And that, perhaps, was
exactly Lee's intention.

Conan's eyes narrowed to obsidian slits. Perhaps it went a
step further: not only to arouse her suspicions, but to serve
as a warning. In that case, the capitalization of the word
"hitch" was explained. It must have been a code word, and
Lee capitalized it to draw Amanda's attention to it. What
would constitute a hitch in their plans? And why did Lee
have to resort to a code word at all? Why not simply tell
Amanda what the hitch was?

Burdened cumulus clouds moved imperceptibly across the
sky from behind him, their shadows marching across the
broad shoulders of War Eagle, while he directed a new scenario on the stage of his mind.

Lee wrote that note under duress, and the agent of the
duress was the hitch in their plans. That's how his gun entered the plot. Amanda said she hadn't seen it in the office,
and that was probably true, but it might have been hidden in
the debris of the struggle. At any rate, it had been in the
office somewhere for Reub to discover later and secrete with
the note in his box, and it had been used to threaten Lee.
The knife wouldn't serve as an effective threat; not against a
big man who didn't shrink at violence. Only the gun would

suffice, and it had been brought to the office by the killer.
Lee had left it behind, forgotten, probably, in a drawer or
closet.

The killer had forced him at gunpoint to write the note,
but Lee had taken matters into his own hands then and in the
resulting struggle disarmed the killer and inflicted the bruises
that the killer later ascribed to an argument occurring *before*
Lee left his house. During that struggle, the killer at some
point found the knife on the desk, and in desperation, in fear,
and in jealous rage, stabbed Lee. It was probably more by
accident than intent that the knife pierced his heart.

And afterward? After Lee fell face down on the floor,
driving the knife deep into his body, the killer undoubtedly
fled the office. But *with* the money?

The money hadn't been left behind. Amanda, who was
the first to enter the office after the murder, would have no
qualms about taking the money if it were there, but she had
Reub to contend with. And Reub didn't take it. Conan was
sure of that now. Reub's behavior both at the time of the
murder and in the last three days made sense now: he was
protecting the killer.

With that in mind, Reub's best course at the time of the
murder would have been to send Amanda on a one-way trip
out of Silver in fear for her life, clean up the office and dis-
pose of Lee's body, and let people assume Amanda and Lee
had run off together, all of which he did. But he would *not*
take the money; a robbery would insure a police investigation, and Reub would avoid that if at all possible. If the
money had still been in the office, he would have put it back
in the safe. But he didn't, which meant the money was already gone. The killer had taken it.

Why? Had it been a deliberate decision? Would the killer
be capable of that after suffering a beating at Lee's hands,
after the shock of stabbing him and seeing him fall to the
floor to lie dead in his own blood? That had been the last
thing the killer wanted.

What *did* the killer want? Why had Lee been forced to
write that note? The answer to that wasn't difficult to fathom.
The killer wanted Lee—without Amanda. The purpose of

the note was to induce her to leave town, then the next step would be to induce Lee to stay *and* to see that he didn't communicate with Amanda until she, thinking he had jilted her, gave him up in disgust. Lee couldn't be kept at gunpoint indefinitely, but he could be blackmailed. The killer could threaten to tell Tom Starbuck that Lee stole the payroll, but to make the threat effective, the robbery had to take place, the killer had to take the money.

But after the struggle, after Lee lay dead, the plan was in shambles, so why did the killer take the money then? To make Lee's death seem the result of an encounter with a burglar? Possibly, but Conan suspected it was simply a reflex action carried out with no conscious thought at all. Later, the killer had no choice but to keep the money; to admit possession of it would be to admit murdering Lee.

The problem with this scenario was that everything about it fitted perfectly with the known facts. Conan examined the perfection of it and felt physically ill. Even the conspiracy between Reub and Adler was explained: they were both trying to protect someone they cared about, and trying to protect Delia from learning the killer's identity. Reub had probably witnessed the murder itself through the office window, and Adler, although he wasn't on the scene, had still seen something, probably the killer following Lee to the office on foot.

And why had Amanda Count come back to Silver?

That was explained, too, but Conan couldn't predict her intended course of action specifically. He was only sure that recovering the note from Reub was very incidental to her plans.

The clouds had marched across the sky until only one streak of blue was visible behind War Eagle; the wind swept fitful whirls of white dust down the slope of the tailings. Conan rose and stood with his hands in fists at his sides, and he wanted to send curses echoing into the silent mountains. The misspent emotions, the years, the *lives* wasted, and the slow acid erosion of a life was as cruel as the sudden ending of it.

No good is going to come of all this, Dexter Adler had predicted, and he was right. But the tide of events was beyond his control, and Conan's presence was irrelevant to that. The key to the sequence of events already set in motion here was a factor that Adler probably wasn't even aware of.

Amanda Count had come back to Silver City.

Conan was in no hurry about returning to the Starbuck house, and even when he reached the crab apples he made an excuse for further delay by checking his car. It was garlanded with fallen blossoms. He turned and saw Delia standing on the porch. She waited until he joined her, and there was in her eyes a pensive longing as she looked out over the town. The scent of lilacs was sweet on the air.

She said, "You must have brought the rain with you from Oregon."

"Well, I guess I'll have to take it back with me when I go."

She turned, one eyebrow raised. "When will that be?"

"Tomorrow. Delia, I'm afraid . . ." He stopped, staring at the neck of her dress; she'd had her apron on when he'd seen her previously today, and it had covered the brooch pinned on her bodice. A cameo, mounted in gold filigree, with a female head in profile. It was the mirror image of the one in Reub's box. That one had faced left; this one faced right.

"Conan? What's wrong?"

He recovered himself and mustered a smile. "Oh, I was just admiring that brooch. A family heirloom?"

She looked down at it and smiled. "Yes, I guess you could call it that. It belonged to my grandmother, Oreana Becket. She was quite a character; typical pioneer woman, but a lady to her fingertips. I wear this thing so often, I'm surprised you haven't seen it before."

"I'm sure I would've noticed it." Then he added, "You seldom see cameo of that quality any more."

"No, I suppose not. There are two of these, actually; a

matched pair. Grandma gave one to me and the other to Clare on our eighteenth birthdays.''

He nodded. A perfect fit; everything such a damnably perfect fit. Delia went on absently, ''I don't know what Clare did with hers. Haven't seen it for years. It's probably hidden away in one of her jewel boxes; she's such a pack rat. Now, what's this about you leaving tomorrow?''

''Well, I'm sorry, Delia, and it galls me to have to admit it, but I've come to a dead end on this case. It's no use going on with it. It's a cold scent; forty years cold.''

She didn't respond to that for some time, only studying him with a faint frown. Finally, she looked out toward Florida Mountain. ''You're right, of course, and it was foolish of me to think anybody could get to the bottom of this thing after so long a time. You gave it your best, I know, and I appreciate that.''

Conan was surprised that she accepted his resignation with such equanimity. He didn't expect argument or recrimination from her, but he did expect more questions.

She seemed to sense that and turned to face him. ''Conan, it meant a lot to me to clear Tom's name, but I care more about the living than the dead. I didn't realize what a hornet's nest I'd be stirring up when I asked you to come here. Now . . . well, it just doesn't seem so important who killed Lee. That's for the past. You know, that's the trouble with living in this town; you can't get loose from the past. It's all around you here; even the very air you breathe is old.'' Then her lucid eyes warmed with her smile. ''Thanks for coming, Conan. Thanks for trying so hard.''

He was at a loss for a suitable reply, and he hadn't found it when the front door opened, and Clare came out on the porch. She was made up and perfumed with a more than usually liberal hand and dressed as if for a special occasion in a dress of ruffled lawn with a faded silk rose at her bosom, and she seemed a wistful Ophelia grown old.

She greeted him with a pretty smile. ''Good afternoon, Mr. Flagg.'' Apparently, she had forgotten that on their last meeting she had tearfully wished for his departure.

"It's so nice of you to drop in on us again. I do hope you'll stay for supper."

He said, "Thank you. Yes, I'll be staying for supper."

"Oh, good. We're having strawberry shortcake for dessert." She opened the door, and as she fluttered back into the house added, "That's Lee's favorite dessert . . ."

...... you to drop in on us again, 1 do
.... you. Yes, I'll be staying for su
.....ou're having strawberry shortc

CHAPTER 18

The tracery of the fretted arch flickered black against strobe-light flashes of lightning. Still testing, it seemed, hiding behind the clouds, light echoing from one turbulent mass to the next. The thunder was ten seconds in coming, a formless rumbling; the wind, laced with fine droplets of rain, howled an obbligato. Conan stood at the balcony railing, his cigarette sheltered in the curl of his palm, face tilted up to the sky.

Within the house, a clock chimed midnight, but the sound was faint against the wind; the old house creaked and rattled with every wayward gust. Conan was still fully dressed, and he doubted he'd sleep well this night, if at all. Delia and Clare had retired three hours ago, but he had spent most of those hours here at what he was beginning to think of as his sentry post, or silently touring the house by flashlight, checking to see that all the doors and windows were locked. He didn't know exactly what he was securing them against, what he was expecting, and that only made the waiting harder. Ultimately, he was looking forward to nothing but the dawn, but at the moment that seemed too far away to fix his hopes upon. He satisfied himself with a closer objective: he was waiting for the storm to break.

A bright, jagged line split the black sky down to the topmost ridge of Florida Mountain. He hadn't reached a count of five before the thunder came bounding across Silver to War Eagle and back again. The rain, chill on his face, beat faster, and he smiled. That was more like it. He felt for the ashtray on the railing and put out his cigarette. Perhaps he should light a lamp in his room so it would be obvious that he was awake and standing guard. No. A light would only serve to blind the guard.

Another white bolt danced briefly, awesomely, over Potosi Peak; the thunder was only four seconds behind it and this time had an authoritative crack. He felt his way to the door, arm extended. The rain was coming harder, and the wind was definitely cold. He needed his jacket.

He found it in the dark and pulled it on as he returned to the balcony, pausing to make sure the flashlight was still outside by the doorjamb where he had left it. Lightning flared again as he crossed to the railing, and there he stood frozen, eyes straining into the darkness.

He had seen something moving on the road below.

Thunder rolled down the valley, then a new flash, and he saw it again: a figure hurrying away from the house toward the school. He spun around, scooped up his flashlight, and by its light made his way downstairs. But he flicked it off when he went out the front door, delved in his pocket for the key, and locked the door behind him. He reached out with his right hand as he crossed the porch, found the post, then the banister, and used that to guide him down the steps, then proceeded haltingly across the rough ground toward the road, hoping for lightning. It came when he had nearly reached the crab apples, illuminating a snow of wind-plucked petals, and ahead near the school, the hurrying figure.

He took advantage of the next flash of lightning to run a few yards down the road; the footing was treacherous, the rain slicking the raw granite. The nightwalker was at the front corner of the schoolhouse now. Conan stumbled and went down on his hands and knees, swearing aloud as he got back to his feet. He'd nearly dropped his flashlight and succeeded in disorienting himself.

Give me some light, damn it. And he almost laughed when a forked bolt obligingly ripped across the sky, throwing everything around him into etched relief. The hurrying figure was still ahead, turning south at Morning Star Street. Thunder rumbled as he pushed forward into the wind. He guessed he was near the corner when he saw a light to his left. The nightwalker had waited until the row of houses on the east side of the street would hide the flashlight from anyone watching at the Starbuck house. Conan followed the tiny, bobbing gleam, moving in fits and starts, reorienting himself with each flare of lightning.

Just before he reached the Masonic Hall he stopped. His quarry was apparently taking the long way around by the bridge. He waited until the bobbing light disappeared behind the bulk of the building, then chanced using his own flashlight as he turned right through the wind-tossed willows on the short-cut across the creek. He didn't waste time trying to stay to the stepping stones, only gritting his teeth as the frigid water splashed over his calves. Once past the creek, he turned off his flashlight, depending on the electric cataclysms in the sky. He had nearly reached the back of the store when he saw the sustained spark of the nightwalker's flashlight above him on Jordan Street and still some distance to the south. He took advantage of another spate of lightning to get behind the store, and there, where its light would be hidden from the nightwalker, turned on his flashlight and made his way toward the open space between the store and the hotel. It seemed to take an inordinate amount of time, but when he reached Jordan Street, his quarry was still moving toward him from the south.

Conan pressed against the wall of the store, watching the approach of that bobbing light. He knew what—and even whom—he was pursuing; the only reason for his pursuit was that he didn't know his quarry's purpose in this nocturnal excursion. Yet at the moment, with the wind howling out of the darkness, with the very existence of a real world in doubt except when it was limned in jarring explosions of light, he

wasn't sure he'd be surprised if that bobbing beam revealed
itself to be an incorporeal phenomenon of the storm.

But it was quite corporeal. It was nearly abreast of him
when a series of three flashes revealed its tangibility, as well
as the identity of the nightwalker. Amanda Count. The hood
of her jacket was up, but as she passed Conan, a gust of wind
threw it back. Her hair seemed black in the white glare of
lightning; no blonde wig tonight.

She passed without seeing him; he remained motionless
against the building. The question of her purpose still wasn't
answered. She couldn't be carrying anything larger or more
menacing than her small handgun. Conan moved to the wall
of the vault to watch her as she went straight to the hotel's
front door, opened it carefully to avoid ringing the bells, then
slipped inside and closed it behind her.

Conan stood encompassed in darkness, face and hair
drenched with the rain that came in driving sheets now, his
pulse quickening with apprehension.

Why had Amanda braved this storm to go to the Starbuck
house?

He turned, putting his back to the wind as he started down
the steep slope between the buildings, and it was then that
he saw a distant, snaking ribbon of yellow light.

Fire. The Starbuck house—it was afire.

A triple-tongued bolt streaked over War Eagle, and in its
quivering flash Conan saw the house clearly; the ribbon of
flame was halfway up the northeast corner of the parlor wing.
Thunder pounded the ground beneath him as he started down
the slope, then abruptly about-faced.

Help—he had to get help. . . .

He ran for the hotel, footfalls thudding on the planks of
the porch. The door was locked; he pounded at it, the shivering jangle of the bells ringing against a new barrage of
thunder. *"Jake! Jake Kulik!"* A pair of lights glared out of
the darkness to his left, beams sweeping up the front of the
building.

A car. Conan ran toward it, waving his arms, and when it
skidded to a stop, heard a shouted inquiry. "What's wrong
here?"

Sheriff Andy Newbolt. Conan didn't have time to wonder at his opportune arrival. "Sheriff, the Starbuck house is on fire! I'm going—"

"Who are—Flagg?"

"Yes. Get some help. I'm going back to the house!"

Newbolt reached for the dashboard and hit the siren. "What about Delia and—" But Conan was already sprinting toward the opening between the buildings. He plunged down the slope and ran for the creek, cursing the slippery stones as he sloshed across it, while behind him Newbolt's siren screamed the alarm. He pushed through the willows up to Morning Star, wet branches slapping at his face. Then a clear run. The wind seemed to take the breath out of his open mouth, and his muscles ached at the demand made on them in the thin, high-altitude air. By the time he turned the corner at the schoolhouse, the yellow ribbon was fanning out and reaching for the roof. Conan drove his heavy limbs forward, his heart hammering. The road's ruts and potholes were canyons and cliffs in the weaving circle of his flashlight. When he reached the crab apples, he saw another flashlight moving toward him. Dex Adler, a shadow figure emerging into the sulfurous glare of the fire.

Conan shouted, "The generator! Get it on—and the water pump! I'm going after Delia and Clare!"

Conan didn't wait for Adler's reply, nor when he reached the front door did he pause to find the key in his pocket. He bludgeoned the glass out with his flashlight, reached through the jagged frame and opened the door from inside, then kicked it back and ran through the sitting room to the hall. A ruddy light shone from within the parlor; the fire was breaking through the north wall. An acrid fog of smoke billowed into the hall. He heard cries from above and took the stairs three at a time. In the upper hall, his light struck two figures ghostlike in long gowns and robes, pale hair falling loose. Delia was shepherding Clare toward the stairs. "We'll be all right, Clare, just don't—Conan! Oh, thank the Lord . . ."

"Come on, Delia—hurry!" He held the flashlight on the stairs while they started down, Clare whimpering and clinging to her sister. A tinderbox, he thought grimly; this historic relic was one huge tinderbox, every piece of wood in it a century dry. He recognized the grinding murmur: the fire eating at the walls. The beam of his flashlight was webbed in smoke, and when they reached the foot of the stairs, Clare began choking and coughing.

"Hold your breath!" he ordered, pushing them on to the sitting room. Light shone through the open front door. Newbolt's car was parked outside, its headlights fixed on the house, double bars shaped by captured rain and smoke. More headlights gleamed from the road; a pickup careened to a halt beside Newbolt's car, and Jake Kulik, his son, Bill Cobb, and Laurie Franklin piled out. With shouts and gestures, Newbolt sent the men around to the north side of the house, while Laurie took Clare in hand and helped her and Delia to the shelter of the trees.

Conan caught Newbolt's arm. "Can you get any kind of real help here?"

Newbolt's face was grim in the frenetic light. "I radioed Homedale and Marsing. It'd take more than an hour to get a fire rig up here."

He didn't have to add that it would be too late by then. Conan turned away and headed for the north wing. There in the carmine glare of the fire, Dex Adler commanded the counterassault on it. John Kulik was on a ladder against the wall of the rear wing, playing a stream of water from a garden hose on the flames engulfing the north wing, while his father was on the ground manning another hose, and Bill came swaying around the corner from the back of the house with two sloshing buckets.

Adler called to Conan, "Delia and Clare—are they—"

"They're out. Around in front. What can I do?"

Adler had a shovel in his hand, but as he turned toward the house, he threw it down; his angular face was slack with hopelessness. "Oh, God, I don't know. . . ."

Conan nodded numbly. Garden hoses and buckets. The fire roared its disdain for those pitiful efforts, curtaining the walls, warping the corrugated metal on the roof. Even the torrents of rain didn't deter this ravening beast, and the wind only goaded it on, driving tentacled sheets of flame before it.

Adler shouted, "John, Bill—get away from that wall!"

A dull rumble sounded from somewhere behind the house; it might have been thunder. Jake Kulik cried, "The water! There's no more water!"

Adler grimaced. "Generator blew. Come on—all we can do is try to save some of the furniture." He led his erstwhile firefighters to the front of the house and directed the evacuation of the furniture out the front door. Conan doggedly hefted and carted with the others, joining the harried parade moving in and out of the smoke and glare. Chairs, tables, lamps, chests, armfuls of silver and china—it all seemed sardonically futile. He saw Lettie Burbage, wet hair plastered down on her forehead, go out the front door clasping a potted plant as if it were the crown jewels. Maggie and Vern Roseberry were there, too, Vern's face an apoplectic pink, Maggie's puffy cheeks streaked with tears and soot. The heat was as blinding as the smoke, the volume of sound staggering. The fire bellowed its jubilance, until at length Newbolt called a halt to the salvage operation.

The defeated salvagers, with Conan trudging wearily in their wake, retreated toward the trees where they huddled like refugees in sodden coats and jackets over a motley of pajamas, nightgowns, and robes. Their eyes were fixed in a consistent attitude of bewilderment on the conflagration, all oblivious to the storm; its savage bolts and temblors seemed feeble against this storm of fire. It had totally engulfed the back and north wings now, and every window was orange. Fountains of embers and burning splinters rocketed on the roaring updraft, and the flames lighted a roiling pall of smoke. The harsh smell of it made breathing an effort even on the leeward side of the wind. The salvaged furniture was piled under the trees, forlorn and at the mercy of the rain, strewn with fallen blossoms.

Delia slumped on the fender of Conan's car clutching a man's jacket around her. It was Adler's, apparently. He stood nearby, his soaked, soot-smeared undershirt clinging to his bony torso, but he didn't seem to feel the chill rain. Delia gazed bleakly at the fire, eyes reflecting the turbulent light. Conan glanced around at the numbed observers, noting absently that Laurie was weeping, and that Reub Sickle wasn't among them. That seemed odd until he considered that even if Reub had heard Newbolt's siren alarm, it would take him some time to reach Silver from his cabin. At the moment, Conan was more concerned with another absence.

He leaned close to Delia, but even then she didn't at first seem to hear him.

"Delia, where's Clare? Delia?"

She frowned vaguely. "Clare? She's right . . . here. Oh, my God!" She surged to her feet, hands pressed to her streaming hair. "Clare, where are you? Oh, *no*—the house . . . she must've gone back to the house! *Clare*!"

Conan left it to Adler to restrain Delia. He ran for the house, pounded up the porch steps and through the front door. Within it, he felt as if he were caught in a cyclonic vortex of heat, as if it would pull him off his feet. He swayed toward the hall, his eyes registering nothing but black and incandescent-yellow abstractions obfuscated with glowing curtains of smoke. He pulled his rain-saturated shirt up and held it over his mouth and nose.

The parlor was a glare of searing light, the hall a Stygian well, but the fire hadn't reached it yet; the stairway was still clear. He shouted for Clare, but he could barely hear himself for the furious din. There was no way to guess where she might be, and even as he stood undecided, the door under the stairs into the kitchen hall seemed to disintegrate, the furnace behind it blustering savagely.

His eyes ran with tears at the acid assault of heat and smoke. He climbed the stairs, shouting through fits of coughing, "Clare! Where are you? Clare?"

The only answer was a shriek of outraged timbers and a prolonged crash. But the stairs were still solid under his feet. He reached the landing, but there stumbled and fell. From somewhere near him came a faint cry. "Help . . ."

"Clare!" She was huddled in the corner of the landing, hair in a turmoil, face contorted with spasmodic coughing. Her arms were folded oddly across her bosom, clutching something against her; something flat and rectangular. He didn't take time to see what it was.

"Clare, can you walk?" He pulled her to her feet, but she sagged limply, only repeating her weak cry for succor. Yet she wouldn't relinquish whatever it was she was carrying.

He picked her up, putting his shoulder against the wall for balance and guidance, and started down the stairs, holding his breath against the smoke, wondering whether the trembling he felt was his taxed muscles or the stairway on the verge of collapse. Voices below him, shouting his name; figures materialized out of the caustic fog. Newbolt and someone else. Jake Kulik. They took Clare from him, and he staggered against the banister, one hand clutching at the newel-post, and briefly, with trenchant clarity, he remembered the sheen given it by generations of hands, and his would be the last to touch it.

"Come *on*, Flagg!" Newbolt was pulling at him. From the dining room came the crash of splintering glass; the windows blown out by the heat. Conan stumbled through the hall and the sitting room to the front door, then across the porch until he caught the post. There he paused, pulling in gasping breaths of chill air.

"You all right?" Newbolt was still at his side.

Conan nodded, and when he could speak, said, "Thanks for coming after us."

"Sure, but this is no place to stop and rest."

The heat seemed to follow them into the rain, and Conan's eyes were so inflamed that at first he thought he was still immersed in smoke. But that cleared enough as he crossed to the crab apples so that he could see Clare sitting on the Jaguar, sagging against Delia, with Adler hovering near. Clare was conscious, if incoherent, her arms still folded protectively over the object—

Conan rubbed at his eyes. Everything seemed hazed in errant lights. Clare was clutching an old-fashioned, leather briefcase, and she wouldn't let go of it even when Delia and Adler got her to her feet, and Adler called to Newbolt, "We're taking her over to my place."

Newbolt nodded. "I put in a call for an ambulance—"

"No! Don't let her get away! She has it!"

Delia and Adler, with Clare supported between them, had already started for his house, but they stopped at the sound of that strident voice. Everyone turned, staring at the figure that appeared, as if brought into existence by the dire light, near the last crab apple tree. A woman with the hood of her jacket thrown back, rain-black hair streaming into a white face in which her dark eyes seemed a demonic invention.

Conan doubted anyone here recognized Mimi Bonnet, and only he recognized Amanda Count.

No. Someone else recognized Amanda. Clare loosed a shrill scream.

Conan shouted, "Adler! Get her out of here!"

"No—damn you!" Amanda started toward Clare, but Adler and Delia were hurrying away with her, while she struggled irrationally, still screaming.

Newbolt grabbed Amanda's arm and spun her around. "What the hell is goin' on here?"

"Stop her! You've got to—she has it! The proof!"

"Lady, I don't know what you're—"

"The *proof*!" she repeated, shrieking the word, the tendons of her neck strained. "The briefcase—she has the—"

"Amanda!" Conan was suddenly gut angry. He gestured toward the clamoring inferno behind him. "Damn it, isn't that revenge enough?"

She glared at him, lips drawn back from her teeth, then spat out, "*No*! That's not enough! I want *justice*!" She twisted out of Newbolt's grasp and stumbled after Clare, whose piercing cries never stopped. And Amanda screamed, *"I want justice!"*

The ridgepole of the house groaned and collapsed in a roaring avalanche, flinging up an explosion of sparks and flaming embers, and only Amanda wasn't distracted by that awesome convulsion. She lunged for Clare, hands outstretched, fingers spread in a raptor's reach. Adler pushed her away, and she fell back with a guttural cry, fell with an odd jerking motion to the ground.

Conan stared at her. It didn't make sense, the way she had fallen; there was something wrong about it. Something wrong about the way she lay motionless now, the rain beating at her face, descending embers extinguished like snowflakes melting when they struck her rumpled clothing. Clare's cries faded as Delia and Adler hurried her toward his house.

Conan was the first to reach Amanda, but Newbolt was close behind him, demanding, "What happened? What in God's name *happened*?"

She was dead, and the dark patch on her bosom was an exit wound. Conan reached that conclusion because now he knew where the bullet had come from. He hadn't heard the report, not against the deafening crash of the house's collapse, but now he saw Reuben Sickle, his rifle cradled on one arm, limping out of the darkness beyond the trees. He moved at a solemn, measured pace, his posture sternly erect, his scarred face reflecting grave regret. Sheba followed at his heels, tail down and ears back.

Reub stopped a pace away from the body and looked down on it. Then he asked, "Sheriff, did I kill her?"

Newbolt's jaw went slack. Finally, he nodded. "You killed her, Reub. Why?"

Reub looked past Newbolt to the fire, and his clear blue eyes seemed the only thing left on this night of disaster that remained as a testament of summer skies and gentleness. He said, "You saw her. She was goin' to kill Delia."

"Delia?" Newbolt frowned. "But she—"

"Revenge, Sheriff," Conan put in quickly, with a glance at Reub. "This is Amanda Count. I guess since Tom is dead, she decided to revenge herself on Tom's widow."

Newbolt considered that, then shrugged irritably. "For Lee Langtry's murder? Damn, the man wasn't *worth* revenging."

Conan nodded, staring at the rain-spattered face of Amanda Count. "Probably not, Sheriff, but she loved him."
. . . *the only beautiful thing that ever happened to me in my life* . . . Then Conan looked up and met Reub's eyes. "It's amazing what people will do out of love."

CHAPTER 19

Conan stood on Dex Adler's front porch and watched an ambulance lurching off down the road. Clare had been diagnosed by the paramedic as in shock and possibly suffering from a mild stroke. Delia rode with her.

Amanda Count's shrouded body waited at the hotel for the arrival of another ambulance. Conan wondered where she would be buried.

He looked at his watch. There was ample light here: bright, white, electric light. Adler had started his generator since his house had become an informal disaster relief headquarters. Two-fifteen. It was all over now, as Lettie Burbage put it, but the shouting. She and the other townspeople had returned to their homes. Dry clothes and other necessities had been provided for the survivors, the salvaged furniture moved into Adler's spare room, offers of assistance and reassurance reiterated. Even Sheba had been offered a temporary home at the hotel. So had Conan Flagg.

There was no wind behind the rain that pattered lightly on the porch roof; the storm had spent itself and the fire nearly so. The chimneys surmounted a black ruin where the last flames fought over the remains, and it was only now that

168

Conan began to realize the full scope of the loss represented
in that hideous pile. The ghost of Asa Starbuck seemed to
take shape in the whorls of smoke. The piano that had come
around the Horn to Silver was gone, the Tiffany-shaded
lamps, the exquisite Kirman, the handmade spread on his
bed, the nickel-plated cookstove, the Waterford crystal and
Coleport china, the irreplaceable books and photographs,
even the jars of strawberry jam that had only yesterday been
stored away for the coming winter. A piece of history was
lost here, and Conan was beginning to understand Silver City
and why its survival was so important.

And more was lost: a home. A home in a sense few people
living now had ever experienced.

Conan closed his eyes and leaned against the roof support,
wondering absently when he had ever felt so exhausted, mentally and physically, or so miserably wet and cold, and wondering if he couldn't have prevented this somehow. Perhaps
he was only salving his sense of inadequacy in thinking that
Amanda Count's determination would have shaped this end
whatever he did.

Newbolt's car was parked a short distance away where the
light from the porch limned the star on the door. A shadowy
figure waited in the back seat. Reub Sickle.

Conan heard voices at the door behind him and turned.
Newbolt and Adler emerged. Newbolt was saying, "Let me
know about Clare, Dex. Anything I can do, just holler."

Adler nodded. "Thanks, Andy. Jake called Delia's daughter—she lives down near Nyssa. Kathleen and her husband
are going to meet us at the hospital in Homedale."

"You're drivin' down tonight? Well, be careful. That
road'll be tricky after all this rain." Then he touched the
brim of his hat with his fingertips as he nodded to Conan.
"Mr. Flagg. You got a place to stay tonight?"

"Jake Kulik is putting me up. What about Reub? Will you
book him?"

Newbolt looked toward the car, frowning. "Don't have
much choice on that. It'll mean a trial, but I don't figure it'll
go hard for him. I hope not, anyhow."

"So do I," Conan said dully, trying not to think about

Reub Sickle in prison; it would kill him as surely as his bullet
had killed Amanda Count. "Sheriff, just out of curiosity,
what brought you to Silver tonight?"

Newbolt gave a short laugh. "We had a call from Laurie
Franklin at the hotel. Said there was a gang of motorcycle
toughs in town squirrelin' around and tearin' up the place."

"A call from *Laurie*?" No, not from Laurie. That call
could only have come from Amanda, who wanted the sheriff
on hand when Clare's guilt was revealed in the contents of
the briefcase.

There was galling arrogance in that, a manic daring in
engineering a disaster on the basis of an assumption about
Clare. But the assumption had proved itself.

Newbolt went on, "I asked Laurie about that call. She
never made it. Don't suppose we'll ever know for sure who
did." He eyed Conan speculatively. "Probably a hell of a
lot about this whole thing we'll never know for sure. Well,
I'd better get goin'. Stop in at the courthouse before you leave
the county, Mr. Flagg. I'll need a statement."

"I'll stop tomorrow on my way home."

Newbolt nodded, then resettled his Stetson and walked out
into the rain to his car. Adler turned to Conan, sighed, and
said, "You'd better come inside."

There was a fire in the hearth. Adler offered him a blanket,
then motioned toward the armchairs facing the fireplace.
"Get yourself warmed up. And I don't know about you, but
I could use something to warm me up on the inside." He
went to the kitchen, returned with two glasses and a fifth of
Jack Daniel's, and put them on the low table between the
chairs. He didn't bother about a chaser as he poured the
whiskey, and after handing one glass to Conan, slumped into
the other chair and stared into the fire. "I used to like watching a fire. I mean, like this, in a fireplace. Don't know if I
ever will again."

Conan pulled the blanket around him and tasted the whiskey; it burned his smoke-seared throat. He studied Adler
silently and didn't find his change of attitude surprising. Adler had not only experienced a great deal in the last two
hours, but had undoubtedly learned a great deal.

Finally, Conan asked, "You have the briefcase here?"

Adler nodded, still staring fixedly into the fire, then after a moment he rose and went to a bedroom. When he returned, he put the briefcase on the table. "I figure you've got a right to see this."

The briefcase was gray and crackled with age, the metal catches pocked with corrosion. Conan wondered where Clare had kept it all these years. Somewhere in her room, probably, so well hidden Amanda hadn't found it when she searched the room. And probably so well hidden in Clare's muddled mind that she had herself lost it until faced with a crisis whose terrible reality forced her to remember. But why hadn't she simply let the fire destroy this evidence of her guilt—the proof, as Amanda called it? That would have been a rational choice, one that might have killed, finally, the beast of guilt and remorse that lived within her, but the beast wouldn't permit its own demise.

Amanda had understood that very well, and had used it. But she'd been driven by her own beast.

Adler pried the recalcitrant catches back, then emptied the contents of the briefcase on the table. It made a small mountain of paper-banded bundles of twenty- and fifty-dollar bills. Two other objects fell to the table with a metallic clink. One was a gold wedding band. Conan leaned forward to pick up the other: a pocket watch on a heavy chain. A Greek key design was incised on the case.

All our anniversaries would be golden. Conan put the watch down beside the ring. "Lee didn't have these with him when he was killed. He must have left them at his house."

Adler nodded. "Don't know why Clare kept 'em with the money, but it's hard to figure how her mind worked. But I'm sure of one thing: she couldn't have killed Lee except in self-defense."

"I know. You saw her follow Lee to the office that night, didn't you?"

"Yes. Then the next day I found a stain on the floor in Tom's office. I suppose Lettie told you all about that."

Conan smiled briefly. "Yes, of course."

"I didn't know Lee was dead then. It never crossed my

mind that Clare might've killed him. I thought that blood was hers—he practically broke her nose, you know—and I figured it just meant she had a fight with Lee before he and Amanda left with the payroll. That's why I didn't say anything about seeing Clare go to the office. I didn't think she needed to have it brought out in public that she'd been right there when her husband took off with another woman.'' Adler paused, looking into the fire. ''Then when Lee's body turned up last month, I had to change my mind, but I didn't find out for sure what happened till Delia started talking about hiring a private detective. Reub got wind of that and came to see me. He was at the office that night, outside at the window. He saw the whole thing.''

''And disposed of the body for Clare, as well as getting rid of Amanda and cleaning up the office?''

Adler looked at Conan, eyes narrowed. ''Yes. You've got it all figured out pretty well, don't you?''

Conan shrugged. ''What about the note? Clare forced Lee to write that at gunpoint, didn't she, before Amanda arrived?''

''Yes. Reub says you have that note now.''

''No one has it. It was in my room.'' It only occurred to him now that he had incurred losses in the disaster, too, but a few clothes and his specially equipped briefcase seemed trivial; they could be replaced. He added, ''I didn't take the note from Reub, by the way. Amanda did. I found it in her room at the hotel.''

Adler only nodded, then, ''Damn, I can't understand why I didn't recognize Amanda. I *knew* her; saw her nearly every day for two years.''

''That was a long time ago, Dex.''

''A hell of a long time ago. Anyway, Reub told me what really happened the night Lee died. When I couldn't talk Delia out of bringing you in on it, well . . .'' He had to brace himself with some whiskey before he could go on.

Conan concluded for him, ''So, you and Reub formed your rather inept conspiracy to drive me out of Silver.''

''Well . . . yes. I'm sorry about that.''

"It doesn't matter; not now. Dex, did Delia see this?" He nodded toward the pile of money.

"Yes. Soon as we got Clare calmed down and in bed, Delia had to see it. Didn't seem to surprise her, really. All she said was, 'Poor Clare—all these years.' "

That seemed to sum it up. Conan shivered and emptied his glass in one swallow. Strange, he couldn't seem to feel the whiskey, and under the circumstances it should hit him hard. Then he rose and began stacking the bills while Adler put them back in the briefcase.

At length, Adler dropped the ring and watch into the case and closed it. "Don't know what I'm going to do with this money. By rights it should be Delia's and Clare's, but I'd just as soon not have to explain that to the IRS. Oh—there's something else you might be interested in." He rose and reached into his back pocket. "Reub gave it to me tonight. Said Clare should have it. It's hers."

It was the cameo brooch. "Reub found it in the office?"

"Yes. I asked Delia what I should do with it." A smile briefly softened the dour lines of his face. "She gave it to Clare, told her Reub had found it somewhere. Clare . . . well, she didn't really know what was going on, I don't think, and she could hardly talk, but she seemed to recognize Reub's name. Told Delia to give the brooch back to him. She wanted him to have it. It'll mean a lot to him."

"Sometimes I think Clare understands more than she realizes. Well, Dex, you have a long drive ahead of you."

Adler went to the hearth and began pulling the fire apart with a poker. "Wait a minute and I'll drive you down to the hotel. You don't look like you're up to the walk tonight."

Conan laughed. "You may be right about that. Thanks. And I'm glad we ended up on the same side."

Adler closed the fire screen, then turned to Conan with an oblique smile. "Well, I guess we always were on the same side. Sorry it took me so long to see it that way."

CHAPTER 20

Conan lost sight of the Owyhees when he reached Homedale, and he stopped for lunch at Max's Café not because he was hungry, but because he needed to reorient himself. This prosperous little farm town seemed ideal for that, with its shops busily vending their prosaic wares; its wide streets full of cars and trucks, the flow of traffic occasionally interrupted by the passing of a clattering freight train; and the conversations around him in the café concerned with weather, crops, inflation, taxes, and the inadequacies and general damnfoolishness of the government.

And Silver City, that paradoxical Shangri-la hidden in the wild reaches of the Owyhees, began to fade into temporal as well as spatial distance. Not that he would ever forget what happened there last night. He had walked up to view the ruins of the Starbuck house this morning. They were still smoking. But the crab apples bloomed, oblivious, against the hauntingly blue sky, and an eagle plied the winds high over War Eagle Mountain.

When he left Homedale, Conan followed the oasis of the Snake River Valley across the state line into Oregon, and at that point, he began thinking seriously of home, of the house by the sea that was his personal castle, of the Holliday Beach Book Shop and Miss Beatrice Dobie, who would upon his return ask with arch subtlety about the *case*. And Meg—no doubt he'd have to endure at least a day of the Treatment. That Siamese aristocrat did not approve of her minions leaving her, especially Conan, and always evinced her displeasures by haughtily disdaining his every attempt at reconciliation until she was sure the point was taken.

But Conan wasn't entirely finished with Silver City yet. He didn't turn west beyond the Snake, but north, following the green belt of farmland flourishing and nourished by the river's waters. A sign warned him when he was ten miles south of the farm community at Nyssa; he slowed and began checking the mail boxes at the roads leading to farm houses. At length, he found the box marked "James and Kathleen Spalding." He drove down a gravel road toward a rambling house with the spick-and-span look of fresh paint, surrounded by bright flower beds and a well-tended lawn.

The doorbell was answered by the lady of the house. Kathleen Starbuck Spalding, an attractive woman who was handling middle age very nicely, looked so much like her mother that Conan was startled. She apologized for the disreputable state of the house as she led him through the living room—although to his eyes it was spotless—and for the absence of her husband and son, who were at a cattle auction in Payette. She took him out to a terrace where Delia was sitting at a wrought-iron table shaded by cottonwoods. She rose, reaching out for his hand. "Conan, I'm so glad to see you. Are you all right?"

He reassured her on that point, but got no further. He was plied with iced tea, then there were more introductions: Marian Spalding, Delia's granddaughter-in-law; then Hugh, Delia's great-grandson, who, she proudly informed Conan, would celebrate his sixth birthday next week. Hugh, a vigorous towhead, was more interested in his toy rifle than in Conan, but the two Mrs. Spaldings were obviously, if politely, curious. However, the conversation didn't get far past the amenities before Kathleen began making renewed apologies. She and Marian had to go to a cake sale at the Grange;

they'd promised to preside over the sales as well as contrib-
uting their culinary offerings. Hugh was induced to leave his
ersatz lethal weapon on the table, and finally all three departed. Delia sighed her relief and poured more tea for
Conan, then sat down across the table from him.

She put Hugh's toy out of sight on the ground. "I don't
know why people think little boys have to play with guns."
Then she smiled to herself. "Kathy and Marian were ready
to forget the cake sale when I told them you were coming,
but I finally talked them into going, so I'd have you to myself."

He smiled at that and sipped at his tea; like the tea Delia
had served at Silver, it was strong and sweet, a welcome
antidote to the afternoon heat. "Delia, how is Clare?"

She shook her head slowly. "Not good. The doctors say
she had a stroke. Dex had her moved to a hospital in Boise."

"Yes, that's what Sheriff Newbolt told me."

"You stopped by the courthouse this morning?"

"Newbolt wanted a statement. I gave it to him, although
parts of it were somewhat edited."

"I appreciate that. Did you see Reub? Is he all right?"

"Yes, I saw him, and he seems to be all right; he's not too
communicative. Newbolt is sure a judge will go easy on him
when he comes to trial."

"I hope so. Dex is getting a lawyer for him. Oh, you know,
that's something I still can't believe. Reub is such a gentle
man; never killed anything except to eat. I can't believe he
could kill Amanda like that."

"Delia, he was protecting Clare. If Amanda had gotten at
that briefcase and opened it with Newbolt right there—"

"I know, Conan, and . . . well, I'm grateful the truth
about Clare didn't come out. Tom will have to bear the burden of guilt still, and I know he wouldn't mind." For a moment, pent tears glistened in her eyes. Finally, she said,
"Clare didn't even recognize me when I left her at the hospital last night. I mean, this morning. That could change. At
least, that's what the doctors told me. But I doubt it; she
doesn't have any fight left. Never did have much, really. The
only time she ever stood up on her hind legs was that once

with Lee, and what a price she paid." Delia's eyes sought Conan's and she smiled musingly. "You knew she killed Lee when you told me you were quitting the case."

"Yes." He frowned and raised his glass; the droning of insects was like a veil on the windless air. "I suppose I should have told you then."

"Maybe, or Dex should've told me when I decided to look for a private detective. Might've saved a lot of trouble. But maybe not. Amanda would've come to Silver either way." Then she shrugged. "Dex meant well, and what more can you ask of somebody than to do what they think is the right thing? Nobody can see into the future."

"Perhaps that's just as well."

"Probably. What would life be without a few surprises along the way? Lord, I'm beginning to sound like a preacher I once knew, with all this philosophizing."

Conan shook his head in amazement. "If that preacher could still philosophize after going through what you have, he has my utmost admiration. As you do."

She hesitated, studying him with a faint smile that didn't find its way to her eyes; they were shadowed with memories. "Well, Conan, maybe philosophy comes with age. You have to have something to make up for the aches and pains and just in general not being up to what you used to be."

"Delia, what are you going to do now? But I suppose it's a little early for you to make any long-range plans."

"No, it's not. I've had more time to think last night and this morning than you might suppose. Traveling time, waiting time at the hospital. And I had a long talk with Kathleen a little while ago." She pointed toward a small cottage nearly hidden behind a screen of spirea and cottonwoods. "See that house over there? That's where Pete and Marian live, but they're building a new house down the road a ways. Kathy says I can have this house when they move."

Conan busied himself with lighting a cigarette, hoping his reservations weren't apparent, but they didn't escape Delia. "Yes, I know, Conan, I always said they'd have to take me out of Silver feet first; that's the only way I'd go. Never say never. That's another good piece of philosophy. I always said

I'd never put Clare in a nursing home, too, but I'm afraid that's where she's headed. Dex says he knows a couple of good places in Boise. Anyway, if it does work out that way, I'll be closer to her here. I guess . . . remember, once I said something about everything having its seasons? Well, I've come to the end of one season, but it's not the end of me. That came as sort of a surprise. I'm so lucky, Conan, I've still got my mind, and my body's holding up pretty well, and I have enough money so I don't have to worry about that. And I have children who want me. Kathy and Jim have pestered me for years to come live with them.''

Conan said noncommittally, "You *are* lucky, Delia.''

She nodded, waiting until he looked around at her. "You probably think I'm just trying to make the best of things, and I am, but it's not as hard as it might seem. That's something else that comes with age. You get a lot of experience in grief, and you learn that when you lose somebody or something important to you, you *will* get over it sooner or later. I've lost Silver. I won't go back there, not with the house gone. I lived there for sixty years, from the day I married Tom. We raised our kids there, and that's where he died. I'll miss that old house, and I'll miss . . .'' She looked south, as if she could see through the trees, through the hundred miles of distance beyond. "Lord, I'll miss those mountains. They're so beautiful. I never saw a day in all these years when they looked exactly the same. There was always something happening; sunshine and storms, flowers blooming, aspen turning gold, snow falling . . .''

For a moment as she spoke, Conan seemed to catch the scent of high mountain air, that subtle fragrance that could be duplicated or bested nowhere else. He remained silent because he could find no words adequate.

Delia reached out and briefly pressed his hand. "Well, I'll always know they're still there, and I'm sure Kathy and Jim would take me up to Silver for a visit, if I get too homesick. Truth is, those mountains are hard. They never give an inch or care one bit about the people living on them. I'm not really sure I *want* to go through another winter in Silver. You have to be young for that.''

Conan laughed. "You mean under eighty?"

"For me, yes. Besides, a person has to keep a stake in the future. That's the trouble with Silver, you know. Its only stake is in the past, and that's important. The present and the future don't exist without the past. But I've spent enough of my life looking backward. I'd like to spend what years are left to me looking forward, and I just realized that this morning watching little Hugh. I think there's a lot I can teach him."

Conan studied her, wondering if he would have the courage—the grace—to accept so resolutely the cruel and immutable facts of age when he came face to face with them.

"Delia, I hope Hugh is a receptive student. He's a fortunate child to have such a remarkable tutor."

"Oh, dear, that must be the Irish coming out in you."

"Irish, or not, it's true." Then he looked at his watch and rose. "Well, I'd better be on my way. I have nearly four hundred miles ahead of me."

She frowned as she, too, rose. "You're driving all the way today? You could stay here and get an early start in the morning."

"Thank you, but I . . . well, I just want to get home."

She nodded. "Then it's time you started. But before you go, I want to settle your fee with you."

"There's no fee to settle."

"What do you mean? Conan, I hired you to do a job of work, and—"

"Yes, to clear your husband's name—which I did *not* accomplish."

Her eyes narrowed. "If you're feeling sorry for an old woman just because she happens to be out of a house—"

"No, Delia." He laughed at the thought. "I can't imagine feeling sorry for *you* under any circumstance. You know I don't depend on private investigation for my livelihood. That means my time is worth exactly what I choose to ask for it, and in this case I've been amply compensated."

She still wasn't satisfied. "Compensated how?"

He made an ironic bow and said, "By the pleasure of making your acquaintance, ma'am. I couldn't ask for, nor will I accept anything more.'' Then he added, ''And that's final.''

''Your aunt Dolly told me you had a stubborn streak.'' Then she smiled and took his arm. ''The pleasure's been mutual, you know. Come on, I'll walk you out to your car.''

When they reached the XK-E, he paused before getting in. ''Delia, I have a guest room and a marvelous view of the ocean at home. You're welcome to take advantage of both any time.''

She pursed her lips, considering that. ''I never have seen the ocean. Maybe I should.'' But her gaze turned southward toward the Owyhees she couldn't see, and Conan doubted she'd ever take him up on his offer. Cordelia Starbuck was as far from her real home as she would ever want to be.

''Good-bye, Delia.''

''Good-bye, Conan. Keep your stakes in the future.''

He nodded. ''But don't forget the past.''

''You can't. It's always with you.''

He drove slowly down the driveway to the highway, stopping there for a last look back. Delia had already gone into the house and with that it seemed she had irrevocably become a part of his past.

He smiled faintly as he turned onto the highway.

It's always with you.

ABOUT THE AUTHOR

M. K. WREN, a widely acclaimed writer and painter, was born in Texas, the daughter of a geologist and a special education teacher. Twenty-five years ago, she found her soul home in the Pacific Northwest, where she wrote CURIOSITY DIDN'T KILL THE CAT; A MULTITUDE OF SINS; OH, BURY ME NOT; NOTHING'S CERTAIN BUT DEATH; SEASONS OF DEATH; WAKE UP, DARLIN' COREY; and the science-fiction trilogy, THE PHOENIX LEGACY. As an artist, Ms. Wren has worked primarily in oil and transparent watercolor and has exhibited in numerous galleries and juried shows in Texas, Oklahoma, and the Northwest.

Attention Mystery and Suspense Fans

Do you want to complete your collection
of mystery and suspense stories
by some of your favorite authors?
John D. MacDonald, Helen MacInnes,
Dick Francis, Amanda Cross, Ruth
Rendell, Alistar MacLean, Erle Stanley
Gardner, Cornell Woolrich, among many
others, are included in Ballantine/
Fawcett's new Mystery Brochure.

For your FREE Mystery Brochure, fill in the
coupon below and mail it to:

Ballantine/Fawcett Books
Education Department—MB
201 East 50th Street
New York, NY 10022

Name_____

Address_____

City_____State_____Zip_____

12   TA-94